TEXAS

*Every book's a keeper
in this sexy saga of untamable Texas men
and the stubborn beauties who lasso their hearts.*

The *first* time is the charm for
Lu Parsons when she's
TAKEN BY A TEXAN (Desire #1137)
in this delightful miniseries debut, featuring
Keeper ranch hand Rip Morris.

When cantankerous Andrew Parsons winds
up wounded on Keeper land, the victim of
a mysterious shooting, feisty JoAnn Murray
is enlisted to mind—and marry—
THE HARD-TO-TAME TEXAN (Desire #1148).

In **THE LONE TEXAN** (Desire #1165),
Lass Small's 50th book, Keeper heir Tom
becomes the silent shooter's next mark…
and shy Ellen Simpson's happily wedded husband.

~~~~~~~~~~~~~

Now, in **A TEXAN COMES COURTING**
(Desire #1263),
go-it-alone cousin Klyn makes it his mission to find
the shooter plaguing the Keeper clan. But what he
discovers during his search is the woman of his
dreams—and a shocking revelation that
pits family duty against desire.…

Dear Reader,

Welcome in the millennium, and the 20th anniversary of Silhouette, with Silhouette Desire—where you're guaranteed powerful, passionate and provocative love stories that feature rugged heroes and spirited heroines who experience the full emotional intensity of falling in love!

We are happy to announce that the ever-fabulous Annette Broadrick will give us the first MAN OF THE MONTH of the 21st century, *Tall, Dark & Texan.* A highly successful Texas tycoon opens his heart and home to a young woman who's holding a secret. Lindsay McKenna makes a dazzling return to Desire with *The Untamed Hunter,* part of her highly successful MORGAN'S MERCENARIES: THE HUNTERS miniseries. Watch sparks fly when a hard-bitten mercenary is reunited with a spirited doctor—the one woman who got away.

A Texan Comes Courting features another of THE KEEPERS OF TEXAS from Lass Small's miniseries. A cowboy discovers the woman of his dreams—and a shocking revelation. Alexandra Sellers proves a virginal heroine can bring a Casanova to his knees in *Occupation: Casanova.* Desire's themed series THE BRIDAL BID debuts with Amy J. Fetzer's *Going...Going...Wed!* And in *Conveniently His,* Shirley Rogers presents best friends turned lovers in a marriage-of-convenience story.

Each and every month, Silhouette Desire offers you six exhilarating journeys into the seductive world of romance. So start off the new millennium right, by making a commitment to sensual love and treating yourself to all six!

Enjoy!

Joan Marlow Golan
Senior Editor, Silhouette Desire

Please address questions and book requests to:
Silhouette Reader Service
U.S.: 3010 Walden Ave., P.O. Box 1325, Buffalo, NY 14269
Canadian: P.O. Box 609, Fort Erie, Ont. L2A 5X3

A Texan Comes Courting

LASS SMALL

Published by Silhouette Books

America's Publisher of Contemporary Romance

If you purchased this book without a cover you should be aware
that this book is stolen property. It was reported as "unsold and
destroyed" to the publisher, and neither the author nor the
publisher has received any payment for this "stripped book."

 SILHOUETTE BOOKS

ISBN 0-373-76263-1

A TEXAN COMES COURTING

Copyright © 1999 by Lass Small

All rights reserved. Except for use in any review, the reproduction
or utilization of this work in whole or in part in any form by any
electronic, mechanical or other means, now known or hereafter
invented, including xerography, photocopying and recording, or in
any information storage or retrieval system, is forbidden without
the written permission of the editorial office, Silhouette Books,
300 East 42nd Street, New York, NY 10017 U.S.A.

All characters in this book have no existence outside the imagination of
the author and have no relation whatsoever to anyone bearing the same
name or names. They are not even distantly inspired by any individual
known or unknown to the author, and all incidents are pure invention.

This edition published by arrangement with Harlequin Books S.A.

® and TM are trademarks of Harlequin Books S.A., used under license.
Trademarks indicated with ® are registered in the United States Patent
and Trademark Office, the Canadian Trade Marks Office and in other
countries.

Visit us at www.romance.net

Printed in U.S.A.

Books by Lass Small

LASS SMALL

finds living on this planet at this time a fascinating experience. People are amazing. She thinks that to be a teller of tales of people, places and things is absolutely marvelous.

To Debra Robertson, who is perfect.

One

___

The Keepers had owned and protected their western TEXAS land for over five hundred years. Any Keeper asked, replied that with all the damned taxes they'd paid out, the land ought to be theirs.

Twenty-seven-year-old Franklyn Keeper was a cousin to Tom Keeper who was in hospital with a broken leg and arm. It was there that Klyn consulted with his hampered cousin.

Tom was serious and thoughtful as he told Klyn how a bullet, silently fired, had wildly startled his horse.

Tom's shocked horse had bucked so that Tom had been pitched off like a barely stuffed scarecrow. That was how Tom had been hurt. It had been an irritating nuisance.

One way or another, there had always been problems there in TEXAS during the five hundred years the Keepers had been there. The silent bullet that intruded into Keeper land was not amusing. Over long years, the bullets were fired from such a distance that there was no warning sound. The bullet rushed by with a whistle of air…and the bullet was low. Deliberately…low? To kill?

The various Keepers had gone over to the river, which was along the edge of their land on the west side. There, they'd looked for the one who was responsible for the firing. They searched the area and even the town of Pleasant, outside Keeper land, on the west side of the separating river. The silent bullet had been a baffling puzzle for them all.

The Keepers weren't the only victims.

Sometime ago, Andrew Parsons had been one. He'd intruded onto Keeper land, and the silent bullet had killed his horse.

Andrew's leg had been caught under the

horse, and he was trapped there until his faithful dog left to find help.

The help was Tom Keeper who sent the ranch pilot Rip Morris to find the dog's master. They found Andrew Parsons in the nick of time and moved the man to the hospital. They never learned who'd fired the silent bullet, which had crossed Keeper land and killed Andrew's horse.

It was now over two years later when Tom Keeper became the next human victim.

And it was Klyn Keeper who decided the puzzle was one of adventure. More than once, Klyn visited his bed-bound cousin with questions about the odd, silent bullets.

Tom gathered others to his bedside so that Klyn could understand how little they all actually knew. And since the gatherings were at his bedside, Tom got to hear all the local gossip and wasn't as bored.

The time came when Klyn assembled minimal gear and departed for his search. Klyn understood he was not the first to try to find the source of the bullets, but he was determined nonetheless.

He brought along two horses. Skipper carried the gear and food, while Jumper carried Klyn and water. Klyn switched the gear each day and rode the other horse.

Klyn liked being alone. His brothers and sisters were more like the other Keepers. They mixed and took a hand in things and gave opinions. A whole lot of opinions. Klyn found them nosy and quite free with their advice.

His daddy had told Klyn, "Take along one of your brothers or maybe two of them. Don't go out thataway all by yourself."

Klyn had looked at his father and sighed with endurance. He had replied, "Not this time."

Klyn had no intention of taking anyone along, anytime, at all. He didn't want to watch out for anyone else. Alone, he would solve the puzzle of the silent bullets.

North of the Keeper place, he visited along the rim of the area where the bullet had been encountered. There were still hoofprints at the place where Tom's horse had been shocked by the silent bullet.

The incident had been a miracle. Neither the horse nor Tom had been killed.

Klyn dismounted at the place where Tom had been thrown by his horse, and allowed his own horses their freedom. The horses were free to move as they chose, but they'd been trained to stay in sight.

It was interesting to Klyn to see on the ground the other horse prints. Keeper riders had come to the place as they tried to figure out the path of the bullet.

Those hoof and boot prints were in the pattern, but it was simple for Klyn to reject them. The visitors had come there from the ranch house and returned in that manner. The riders had come there to look. To discuss. To know what was happening.

Some had ridden around and looked farther. But none of them had studied the pattern of arrival and departure of what had happened. They'd just been curious.

From all that he'd learned from Tom and from what he saw with his own eyes, the silent bullet was always from the west. Klyn plotted what he believed to be the path of the bullet.

He mounted one horse and went to the place where Andrew Parsons's horse had been shot.

Most of the bones of the dead horse were still where the bullet had dropped the animal. From this location, Klyn figured that the flight of the stunning bullet was identical to the flight of the previous bullet which had struck Tom's horse.

The bullet had to have come from the west, of course, and a slight bit south? It was from the west without doubt. And it was from so far away that no sound of the firing had been heard…unless the firing sound had been smothered in some new and startling manner?

Who was their enemy?

A silencer was not new, but one for such a big gun? Could such a gun have a silencer? Something that fired a humongous bullet? It was very sobering to consider. Had the person or persons moved the gun? Its bullets came the same way along the area. It would be interesting to know why.

With curiosity and care, Klyn rode slowly outside the channel of the potential gunfire. And he watched. He was extremely alert and cautious. He spoke to the horses softly. Oddly enough, that soft murmuring made the horses more alert. They watched around exactly like Klyn. The horses were aware the man was in no hurry.

In time, Klyn and his horses reached the far western part of the Keeper land on the edge of the canyon. Just across the canyon was the town of Pleasant. It was from somewhere around there that the silent bullets originated. In spite of all the other searchers before him, Klyn would find who was the culprit. He would. He had the time and patience.

On the edge of Keeper land, Klyn looked down to the river below. The river had been there forever, and the wide, deep canyon proved the water had wildly flooded many times.

He traveled both ways along the brink, looking down into the canyon for trails. The drop was such that no trails were available. That was interesting.

It took Klyn a while to find a way down to the river. The paths had been made by animals. Some of the paths stopped quite abruptly, and the intruders were scolded by small animals and birds for riding on such a trail with horses, for crying out loud!

Men are territorial. So are creatures. There is no difference between human and creatures in that.

It caught Klyn's attention that the horses moved aside along one portion of the cliff. The horses were both suddenly suspicious of the ground and moved in from the edge. How had they known?

Klyn was smart enough to agree with what the

horses did. He looked around, watching. The land was fragile there. It was interesting that the surface looked okay. But something clued the horses to be careful.

Klyn finally made his way down to the river. So that he could find his way back, he looked around carefully and drew in the awesomeness of the area. It wasn't man who did such marvels.

Klyn wondered how long it would be before the local men changed the canyon to suit themselves. He smiled. At age twenty-seven, he must be a throwback. He was a man who wanted things to stay the same.

As the one horse carried him along, Klyn considered that. So he was stuck in time? He looked around at the vast emptiness of the area and his smile grew wider. With its weeds and trees the rugged terrain at the bottom of the cliffs was the home of all sorts of creatures. There was a rat. Over yonder, almost blended into the new trees, was a deer. There was a lost or escaped bull who watched Klyn with a very hostile, challenging look.

Klyn slowly realized he was invading an area that belonged to other creatures. Sitting his horse with the élan of a man who knew what he was doing, Klyn took off his Stetson and bowed at the various creatures as he told them, "Just passing through."

Even that comment showed how isolated Klyn was that he spoke aloud in these circumstances. It amused him. Was he losing his need for isolation?

As he went along on his horse, watching, his mind considered his aloneness. When had he ever been without human company?

Most of the time.

Why did it now come to his attention?

How many times had his dad said that Klyn's time would come to blend in with all the other peoples? Was the change...there? Naw.

With interest, Klyn crossed the bottom of the washed-out, widened canyon, watching the birds who scolded and the creatures who stood silently as he hustled out of sight. Klyn found another trail that actually took him to the other side of the canyon. The trail was in mostly shallow water and well hidden, and he'd had a hell of a time finding it.

At the top of the far canyon wall, Klyn contemplated the small town of Pleasant. How interesting the town had been given that name... Pleasant. Not Perfect or Lousy but...Pleasant.

The houses and the stores weren't ostentatious, but they were clean and charming.

He would see the sheriff first, Klyn figured as he led the horses carefully into town. People looked at him and nodded in a careful manner. They were courteous and cautious to a stranger.

In a small town, thataway, a stranger was...strange.

Klyn sought out the sheriff's office. The man wasn't there. His not being there was not a surprise to Klyn. He knew sheriffs had too many things to do.

So after identifying himself, Klyn told the deputy, "Sir, I'm looking for something and wonder if you could help me."

The deputy considered Klyn without a smile and said, "Yeah?"

Klyn nodded, then said, "I'm a Keeper from east of here and looking for a particular kind of silent weapon that has to be just about as big as a small cannon."

Other men gathered and listened. They were silent and sober-faced.

They were mostly bored. Anything would interest them.

The deputy said, "We ain't got none of them

there kind of things around this here place. You a Keeper or a salesman?''

Klyn smiled. "A Keeper."

The deputy sighed. "Some of you all've been here before on just this problem."

Klyn nodded. "We need to find the cannon-like weapon that fires across the river's canyon and onto Keeper land. Whatever the weapon is, it sends a bullet over Keeper land from such a distance that we don't hear the firing sound. The bullet is bigger than any gun's. We've found them in dead animals. Here's one I brought along."

The deputy accepted the bullet and looked at it carefully. Then he gave it back to Klyn. The deputy rubbed his face whiskers thoughtfully and mentioned, "I've heard tell of that."

Klyn went on: "There was an intruder on a horse who clipped his way through a Keeper fence. He was trapped for several days with a leg caught under the horse when it was struck down by a bullet. He'd have died right there if it hadn't been for his dog. The bullet was from this direction."

"Yeah. They told us. We looked, but didn't find anything at all."

Klyn went on: "We've another man whose

horse was so startled that it threw the man who broke an arm and a leg.''

The deputy nodded as he said, ''Tom Keeper. We've heard of that.''

Klyn nodded his head seriously and continued, ''We're looking for whoever it is that sets off such a gun. Do you know anything about that?''

The deputy seemed to consider the question with some earnestness. ''No, but we've gone around and asked. We watch.''

''All us Keepers appreciate that. Here's the Keepers' phone number. Call collect. They'd be glad to hear from you.''

''I know.'' The deputy took the card. He read it. ''You're a Keeper?''

''Yes, sir.''

''You Keepers are a good bunch.''

Klyn smiled gently and replied, ''Thank you.''

The deputy nodded a couple of times as he said, ''I'll see what the sheriff says.''

With some drollness, Klyn replied, ''We'd appreciate that.''

The deputy asked, ''Your mama teach you manners?''

Klyn grinned. "My daddy smacked 'em into all us kids."

The deputy and his listeners laughed, then the deputy asked, "You measure the area that the bullets came along?"

"Pretty close."

"That oughtta help. You're making all us curious all over again. I'll go and look around, too."

With that finally mentioned, Klyn said very courteously, "Stay off the actual path over. It's where the bullets go along."

The deputy nodded.

So Klyn smiled and said, "Thank you." Then he mentioned: "I'll be at the hotel. I'll be around for a while."

The deputy nodded.

Klyn tilted the rim of his TEXAS Stetson to the men, and they shifted their feet and nodded in return.

Klyn observed the town with his two strange horses, and attention was drawn to them. Not to Klyn...to the horses.

The TEXAS horse is utilitarian. People don't need fancy creatures to ride. They need something that lasts. But the men were curious about Klyn's horses.

With courteous nods to Klyn, they got off their chairs to move along Klyn's horses as they questioned where he had gotten them.

Needing information about the bullets, Klyn was cordial and patient. He showed off his horses, declined selling either and then began to ask questions.

The men replied, "We don't know of no particular sound of anything being shot off across this here countryside. But a whole lot of shots hit the other side of the canyon."

Klyn nodded.

One of the men inquired of another, "Doesn't Kayed shoot off his cannon every night when he takes down the TEXAS flag?"

Another man replied, "That's local. This dude's looking for something that travels over past the river a ways."

Klyn commented, "I'm hardly a 'dude,' man. We've been hereabouts for over five hundred years." That ought to straighten 'em out.

While the others tilted their heads to observe Klyn more judiciously, Klyn laughed. "In the diaries, it mentions who came when and how. They could write so fancy back then."

So one of the men said, "I'm the editor of the newspaper around these parts. How about letting me copy some of that stuff?"

Klyn replied, "I think my uncle has the papers under lock and key at the bank, but you could come along home with me and I'd introduce you to him. He's a Keeper."

One said, "So he keeps the papers or the diaries?"

Tolerantly, Klyn smiled as he corrected, "That's our last name...Keeper."

Another of the men said, "So you're a Keeper. I've heard tell of you all."

"We're good people. Not one laggard or crook left...that we know."

The men grinned and chortled a bit. Then they began to talk about families. And names.

Slowly, Klyn got them on the topic of guns and then to the silent bullets again.

The men considered the problem. The deputy had joined the group, and he suggested they all think about it for a time and listen for any new information. He told Klyn, "The hotel has ten good rooms. You'll get one easy enough. We'll rack our brains, thinking about this here stuff. And I'll be sure to tell it to the sheriff."

Klyn nodded and smiled kindly.

Another in the group said, "Yeah. Stick around for a while and look us over. We could use some fresh blood around here."

Klyn nodded once more. Then he waited for the end of the welcomings and finally said carefully, "You all've got a good town. But I'm just here for a while. When I find out what's going on, I'll be going back home."

That astonished the group who felt they lived in The Perfect Place...just like all TEXANS do, no matter where they are in the state. They found themselves speechless! That was another shock. TEXANS are *never* speechless. These were! And being unable to exclaim, it gave them another shock!

Klyn simply watched and listened. Who was the one who fired the silent bullets? Where was he in this small river town?

Klyn wouldn't leave before he knew.

Two

In a week's time, Klyn individually sought out just about all the people in Pleasant and talked with them, questioning about the huge bullets that occasionally went east across Keeper land. Nobody knew anything about it, at all, or why it happened.

The deputy suggested Klyn go to the houses closer to the canyon. He pointed in the direction he wanted Klyn to take. "Over thataway. Somebody there might know of something about the big gun."

Klyn looked across the way, and beyond the

canyon toward home, and he nodded. Though he wouldn't leave before his mission was complete, he was anxious to get back home to people he knew.

So Klyn went to the ranch that was about two miles away. He rode his horse alongside the road, which was in perfect repair. TEXAS roads are always thataway.

He arrived at the ranch and rode to the formal building. There, he got down from his horse and went to the front door which was opening. The two men measured each other as they said their names and nodded their heads. Then Klyn Keeper asked Will Still, "Do you know of anybody who fires a hell of a silent big bullet toward the east?"

"Not that I've heard."

Klyn went on, "We've seen the bullets in the bones of some horses and cattle."

Will said, "Come sit down. We shoot a lot of bullets around here. Not that you're in jeopardy, but the people do fire bullets and hit the other side of the canyon. You all Keepers mind that?"

Knowing full well that Tom and the earlier Keepers had dealt with the same question, Klyn said soberly, "It depends on how deep across the land the bullet is fired."

"I can see that."

Klyn asked, "Does anyone have such a long barreled gun to fire a bullet that far?"

Carefully, Will inquired, "How far?"

As Klyn tilted his Stetson back on his head, he told Will, "The distance through the land the Keepers have across the river. The bullets that cross there go back long years. That makes it odd."

Will said, "Ahhh. What all have the bullets killed?"

Patiently, Klyn described it all. The animals hadn't been too many, but more than the Keepers wanted to lose. Then Klyn added: "A dead horse under which a man was trapped for several days, until his dog found my cousin's help. Recently, a bullet grazed the front of a horse's chest, causing it to throw a very qualified rider who broke his arm and leg."

"Ouch."

Klyn nodded soberly and commented, "That's about what they all said."

Will then asked, "How's he coming along?"

"Very well." Klyn smiled. "He's my cousin and getting spoiled. We'll have to retrain him when he's out of bed."

This time, Will nodded.

Klyn squinted his eyes a tad as he said earnestly, "I need to know who the hell is shooting those big bullets over onto Keeper land. It's vital to get such shooting stopped before somebody is killed. Some human."

"I can see your point." Will considered. "Why not talk to one of the women? They know *everything*."

"Who do I contact?"

Will considered as if he was sorting through people. He said, "Wellll…let's see about this. Uhhhh. I know! Get in touch with the young woman who lives with her family."

"Who's that?"

"Her name's Elizabeth Moore." His eyes twinkled. "She's about twenty-three, rigid and difficult. You'll have to be careful with what you say and how, but *she* knows everything around and about. God only knows what all women pass goss—uh, information along to her."

The two laughed as men tend to do.

Will then urged, "Try her. She'll talk your ear off, but you'll hear all the current events."

"Elizabeth Moore." Klyn rolled the name over carefully so that he would remember it. "Where exactly do I go to contact her?"

"Come inside, and I'll draw you a map."

So Will Still drew a map of how Klyn should get to Elizabeth Moore. He explained the goings-on in Pleasant as he went along.

Klyn nodded, but he said, "I'll know it better if you write that stuff on the paper."

Will could understand that, so he talked as he drew and labeled and gave out lineage, who married who and why and where they lived.

It was mostly talk. Klyn would never remember it all. Still, he asked questions and got more information on each person.

Will was a gossip.

Klyn understood that what Will Still told him was what everybody knew so that they could understand each person. People aren't predictable. The smoothest seeming person generally has the biggest burden.

With that silent observation as to what all he was assimilating, Klyn looked more closely at the man who was directing him so fully.

This was how history was garnered in olden times. Word of mouth. Klyn listened more closely so that he could compare Will's stories to those of other people during his search.

With the map and all the sidelines information, indicating people whom Klyn would probably never see, he rode through the edge of town. His horse Skipper was the carrier of him that day. Jumper tagged along with interest.

Around that small town, there were rabbit runs, the perfect roads went gently on by and it was all pretty. The trees were short but full; the slowly chewing milk cows watched him idly.

There were cacti and an occasional dog who stayed back and watched silently as the man passed on his horse with the other horse following.

And there were prairie dogs. Their noses wiggled as they scented the man and the horses.

When Klyn arrived at the other edge of town, he dismounted and walked his horse over to a tub filled with water. He allowed the two horses to drink. While the horses were involved with water, Klyn looked around.

A man ambled over from those who were lounging on chairs in the shade by the stores. The man never took his eyes from Klyn.

Klyn didn't watch the man approach but looked around. He allowed the curious man freedom to turn away if he wanted. The man didn't. He made a beeline to Klyn.

The man asked, "You Klyn Keeper?"

Just the fact that the man had his first name right caused Klyn to say, "Yep."

"Will Still called to say you'd be along, if you was honest." He grinned.

Klyn nodded and commented, "I must be."

That made the man's grin widen. "We'll see." The man eyed the horses and commented, "They look worth the kindness."

"Thank you."

The man then took off his hat so that Klyn could see him better. And the man said, "I'm George Wilkins. We've been watching for you on this side."

"That was neighborly."

"We're glad you're here."

"I need to find out who is firing a very large gun across the canyon and onto Keeper property. We have cattle there. We lost a horse hit with a bullet back a ways in time."

"Ahhhh. I've heard tell of the wind's rushing."

And Klyn asked, "Did you now? What did you hear?"

"That somebody don't know when to quit?"

With seriousness, Klyn added, "Or how to aim?"

"Yeah." The man became thoughtful. "Who do you belong to?"

"The Keepers."

"They're good people. You hired or are you one of them?"

"I'm a nephew to the senior Keeper across the river."

The listener raised his eyebrows and nodded. But he didn't say anything more.

One of the other men had ambled up to hear and said thoughtfully, "The Keepers've been around for a while. They've had the land across the river for a long old time."

Klyn agreed. "Over five hundred years."

That silenced the men.

Then Klyn wondered if he'd made a very serious mistake and someone would hold him hostage? He said, "I've been talking to the deputy. I'm waiting for the sheriff."

The one called George said, "He's a good man. Busy. You'll have to go to his office and just wait. He'll show up, but it might take a while."

Glad to escape the potential visit, Klyn touched his hat brim as he said, "I'm obliged."

One of the other men directed, "His office is by the jail. It's over thataway."

Klyn nodded and again touched his hat brim.

* * *

Klyn walked his horses over to where the sheriff's office was. But first, he took his two horses to another of the town's water troughs. He saw to it that his horses were settled in the shade. The ties were long and loose. The horses mouthed their bits and looked around. They were curious.

Klyn went to the obvious portion of buildings to wait. And the sheriff was there in his office.

His name was Bob White. He was a tough man who watched levelly and spoke his opinions. He asked Klyn, "You a Keeper?"

Klyn smiled. "Yeah."

"You look like 'em. Who's your daddy, boy?"

"Peter."

The sheriff smiled. "I was in school with him. He's a strong, honest man."

"He had a hand swing that young boys dread."

"Best they mind the first time."

Klyn nodded. "We learned."

The sheriff laughed and accepted Klyn easily. He relaxed and asked, "What's troubling you?"

"About what troubles us all over yonder on

the other side of the canyon. It's the silent bullets that come whispering across Keeper land."

Sheriff White nodded seriously. "We've heard of the silent bullets. Matter of fact, my deputy mentioned you were doing some investigating. It has to be people who've been around hereabouts. We've watched and listened. But we haven't caught them...yet."

Klyn asked, "How can I help?"

"Snoop around. Watch. We'll be doing the same thing. The culprit can't remain silent much longer."

"We'll see. Where do I go?"

They got out local maps and pored over them. The phone rang, and the sheriff was distracted, but he came back to the maps every time.

Klyn said, "This has been going on for a long, long time. This is where one of the killed horses was...here. And this is where another was shocked by the speeding bullet that took the hair off the horse's chest. Not one drop of blood, but his thrown rider broke his arm and a leg. He's still incapacitated."

"Yeah." That was sympathy and understanding from the sheriff. One word was enough.

The sheriff then said, "If the trail is logical

and true, the person firing those shots has to be along this line and across the Canyon to...here.''

Klyn replied, ''Yes. I've searched that area, and the people just tell me they don't hear such a shot.''

The sheriff replied, ''We'll see.''

So Klyn was invited to Sheriff White's house for lunch. And Klyn was glad to go. Eating at a restaurant got lonely real quick. The food there had been good, but the invitation to an actual house was just what he needed. He smiled. He was just like any other man.

The sheriff's wife's name was Laura. She opened the door with a big grin, which widened as she saw they had a guest for lunch. She was welcoming and pleased Klyn was there.

She made Klyn laugh. Her husband grinned and watched her like some dog, waiting to be petted.

Laura excused herself and vanished. They could hear her muffled voice in another room. Then there was the clink of the phone being put in its cradle.

Laura busily delayed lunch, but she set another plate at the table. She took her time.

A female arrived. Her name was...Elizabeth

Moore. She wore a white silk blouse and white trousers, but she'd quickly added a skimpy, buttonless, sleeveless black Spanish vest.

Elizabeth looked at Klyn.

He thought with a gasp, This is Elizabeth Moore?

She must have thought her chest was completely covered. She was not...entirely so. The hair on Klyn's neck had oddly lifted. His breathing was strange. He wished the vest would glide just—naw, not with the sheriff there, watching.

Klyn considered the woman. This Elizabeth Moore would gobble him alive. She'd wring any knowledge he had from his brain. She was not an ordinary woman.

Then he admitted to himself that if he was going to die anytime soon, it might as well be with her. She'd suck his blood from him all by herself, but he wouldn't mind.

That odd encounter, there at the Whites' house, was a strange time. Klyn had no memory of eating lunch...but they were to have dessert! The rest of the meal had been removed from the table. Klyn could remember no part of any other food.

The time had vanished in a blip. Klyn found

they were eating ice cream and cookies as he realized again that Elizabeth Moore was really something.

He looked at Elizabeth. Her eyes sparkled. She blushed. She spent a whole lot of time laughing, but she mostly looked at her plate.

It was pretty obvious that Elizabeth had rushed to be there on time. She was conscious of not having on a bra. But she did not call attention to her chest by looking at it. She was under the opinion that the vest was secure.

It was not...entirely. It shifted and revealed the fact that she had no underwear on the top part of her body. She did wear the soft, wicked silk of the pullover, but the black buttonless vest was not an actual covering.

Elizabeth laughed and blushed at Klyn's average comments on the area. He thought that she could have looked at him, too. How come she didn't look at him? Women looked at Klyn Keeper.

And he understood that if Elizabeth actually did turn her face and focus her eyes on him, he'd be turned to stone. It would be better if he avoided looking at her eyes until he'd lain with her and was surfeited by her body, her mouth, those eyes....

What a way to go.

It would be fascinating and very worthwhile to see if she would make love with him. Ahhh. That would be the ultimate experience for Klyn. The inside of his body shivered in anticipation.

Mrs. White seemed satisfied. Was it her good food? Maybe it was that Elizabeth was there?

Klyn helped to remove the dishes. He could look at Elizabeth thataway as he moved around the table and shifted plates. As he leaned over to take her plate, he caught a glimpse beneath the white silk covering her chest. It was a wonder that he could then move at all.

The plates Klyn carried into the kitchen were put on the wrong side of the counter. He didn't notice. He went back to see what else he could take from around Elizabeth.

He was zonked. At twenty-seven? He was acting like a fifteen-year-old male. Maybe twelve.

Well, he'd never before encountered a woman like Elizabeth. A breathtaking female who blushed, for crying out loud.

Most of the females Klyn knew, he'd known from birth. They were charming and very familiar. Just about too familiar. This Elizabeth was different from any other woman he'd ever known. She was magic.

With that, Klyn remembered his daddy telling him long ago, "Beware of women who peek at you, blush and smile. They're dangerous for a man and they generally flirt with any other man around."

Well, a little danger was stimulating for a man. He would see if that wasn't so.

Klyn found that all the things his daddy had warned him about were crowding in on him. Like the simple riding of a horse. Being sure of the horse. Riding a Jeep and being sure of the gasoline. Take a bath before a date and gargling. Taking money along and hiding some of it in the car. Not carrying it all in his jacket.

Then there was getting a date home on time. Having a cell phone in the car if there was any problem. How to handle a drunk woman. How *not* to handle a drunk woman.

Klyn smiled. His brothers and sisters had all been lectured along the way in how to do what all.

So here was a woman who wore no bra but donned a black vest that didn't cover as much of her chest as she expected it would.

Tough.

That "tough" was Klyn's. He had to survive.

In his mind, his absent mother gave him "the look" and his absent father observed Franklyn very intensely. How could Klyn know all that?

And there at the Whites' house, Klyn smiled. He looked down and licked his lips, but he did smile.

At the table, Sheriff Bob White coughed and rubbed his nose and didn't dare look at Klyn again.

Laura White ruled the conversation. She offered subjects. She guided thoughts. She was superb.

So was the neophyte who wore the thin white silk top and the inadequate black vest.

It was then that Klyn realized Elizabeth needed his guidance. Yes. He could allow a couple of days' time or even a whole, entire week in instruction of conduct for an unknowing female. He could allow that. He would be kind and gentle, and she would learn…enough.

Klyn's eyes danced in anticipation. He said to his hostess, "Let me help with the dishes. I have the time."

Laura White lifted surprised eyebrows and replied, "I have a dishwasher. Bob is especially kind." She smiled at her husband.

Bob coughed quite gently, which nicely covered his burst of laughter.

So Klyn said to Elizabeth, "I have two horses. Do you ride at all?"

"I have my car here."

"Oh?" And he was trapped. He had the horses there, and he couldn't lure her off anywhere. So with sudden urging, he said, "We can leave your car here and take a ride down to the cliff. You do know about the bullets that go across Keeper land?"

She looked at him kindly and said softly, "No. What do you mean by that?"

He had her. He shifted a tad and said, "I'll let you see what all I'm trying to learn. I'm not making much headway." He smiled softly and with innocent interest.

She licked her lower lip.

He did have her! She would swoon. He'd catch her and he'd have her! Yeah.

The odd part was that horns didn't sprout from his head like his dad said they would, and his feet didn't turn into goat hooves.

Three

—

With lunch over, they gathered outside. The sheriff said, "We probably ought to let Elizabeth go home."

His wife said, "No."

Klyn said, "I'll take her along, but she ought to ride one of my horses and see what's going on in the canyon."

The sheriff looked at Klyn and asked, "Can you handle that?"

Klyn looked far, appeared thoughtful, then said, "I'll…try."

That made Elizabeth laugh.

Klyn watched her do that. Then he asked permission of the Whites to move Elizabeth's car aside and out of their way, so that Elizabeth could ride one of his horses.

Bob said, "Sure. Put it over on that side. You all coming back anytime soon?"

Klyn said thoughtfully, "We'll see." He'd found a floppy, side-brimmed hat in one saddlebag. It was made of soft leather of a nice brown. It was sewn together with strips of hide. He gave it to Elizabeth.

She smiled just a tad as she opened it with curiosity and put the floppy shade hat onto her head. And she watched a careful Klyn as he realized he'd found what he hadn't been looking for. Elizabeth.

The Whites were riveted as Klyn took some rather large safety pins out of a bag on one of the horses. He proceeded to make a three-pin extension and secured the ends on both sides of Elizabeth's wild and wicked black sleeveless vest, cinching it together.

That only caused Bob to strangle a bit, in hilarious surprise, and he was useless in communication for a while.

But in the meantime, a sober-faced Klyn mentioned, "I have a cellular phone, and we'll be in touch."

Laura White blinked. She looked at Elizabeth and asked, "You okay about this?"

Elizabeth laughed. She blushed. But she was very amused. And she had no comment at all.

That startled Laura. Her attention was more riveted. She watched the two guests with wonder.

Klyn was easy and ordinary. He gave no indication of being hyper or...well...lusting. He just seemed as though he was going to show Elizabeth around a little and be right back.

Klyn helped Elizabeth onto one of his horses. Then he mounted the other horse. With a brief touch to his Stetson's brim, Klyn ushered them off on the horses' lazy jog.

Neither of the shocked Whites had inquired as to Klyn's cellular phone number. They didn't think of that until the two riders were just about out of sight, cantering gently, talking and laughing.

What was so funny? They hadn't laughed like that during lunch! Why were the two strangers so easy with each other, and what were they saying?

Bob and Laura looked at each other blankly.

They'd forgotten what it was like when they'd first met.

The two strangers became friends as they rode along slowly, exchanging observations, figuring what all they'd have the time to see. They came closer to the edge of the canyon, down the middle of which the river moved.

They watched it.

At one place, the water flowed down slight drops and gathered in pools where the depth was chancy. The colors of the sand, the dirt and the water with the reflection of the afternoon sky made it all magic.

It was soothing. Who would ever believe someone could shoot a bullet across that scene to carelessly kill living things across the way? Out of sight, out of mind?

Or was the shooting deliberate? Who would secretly be that sly and mean? What was the purpose?

An enemy of the Keepers?

Klyn looked over at Elizabeth and wondered if he was wise to bring her along in something that could be dangerous. He wouldn't take her down to the area of danger. He'd just keep her with him while he allowed her to decide about him.

He asked her gently, "Who all has guns around here?"

Elizabeth replied, "Just about everybody."

Klyn sighed. "That doesn't narrow it down a-tall."

She grinned.

How could a grin lift a man's heart thataway? Then he saw that she shrugged. She could do that wonderfully. It was too bad he'd used all those safety pins to anchor the opening of her vest. With just her with him, and his horse knowing which way to go, he could have just watched her chest!

Well…darn. He'd changed the expletive in his thoughts because he wasn't used to being with a female. And he needed to watch what all left his mouth.

A jackrabbit, lean and big, burst from the ground and ran dodging, expecting to be hit with a bullet.

Klyn controlled his laugh.

Elizabeth gasped, stood on her stirrups and pointed as she shouted, "Get him!"

Klyn chided, "Now what would we do with

a scrawny rabbit like that? He's all hair and bone.''

She sat back on the saddle. Disgusted, she replied, ''He'd have made a good taste to a pot of soup.''

Klyn was astonished and asked with exaggerated interest, ''You cook?''

She was indignant. ''Of course! And you missed shooting that rabbit!''

He *tsked* as he shook his head. ''That wasn't a bunny rabbit, that was a range rabbit! He was so scrawny that after he was skinned, there'd only be bones.''

To cover her laugh, Elizabeth said, ''Hah!''

So as their horses walked along, looking around and being interested, Klyn and Elizabeth talked and laughed. They went farther than Klyn meant for them to go.

Well, he'd hated to let go of her attention. They talked about everything they could share. Everything from how the land looked, to what all they'd done as children. It had been a bonding. At least, he thought they were bonded. He smiled at her.

She really seemed to enjoy the ride. She told Klyn, ''You have good horses.''

He smiled. He didn't say how lucky he was

to have her to himself. He was content and alert, because she was fascinated by everything.

If they'd been in a car, they would have viewed everything by now and gone back to the Whites'. This way, he could keep her to himself much longer without any interruption but the horses' hooves, the birds chirping, the plane that was a moving dot in the sky and the sound of the river below in the canyon.

Klyn watched Elizabeth. He smiled and told her, "Let me know if you're getting tired. We still have to go back to fetch your car."

She looked at her watch and stopped her horse. Klyn stopped, watching her soberly. She looked around. She breathed deeply. She smiled at him.

That smile sparked sensations inside his body in a very unusual way. When had a woman smiled at him like that? She wasn't flirting. She was simply contented.

He liked it that she was taking pleasure in looking at the scenery. But he wanted her to look at him, too.

She grinned at him and said, "I suppose you'll have to drag me back, kicking and screaming?"

He sat his horse with one hand holding the

reins, his other hand fisted on his thigh. He said softly, "I have a phone. We could call your mother. We have a tent, wood, food and water. We could be here for...four days to a week."

By himself, he could have easily lasted a week out here. But he could hunt. He had guns. There was a river to fish.

She grinned as she shook her head. "Don't lure me. I have a date tonight. It would be rude of me to stand up a nice young man."

His face became stolid. He said, "Oh? Who is he?"

She replied casually, "An old friend."

"Where you going?"

She smiled and looked beyond him. "That cliff is odd. That must be the bullet-battered place."

She'd distracted him. He looked across the canyon. He said, "Some of the face of the cliff must have fallen. There is no growth on its front."

Elizabeth guessed, "Water?"

He looked at her curiously. "Water...?"

She shrugged and said, "Either water over the edge or inside the cliff." And she echoed his comment. "There's no growth there, on the face of the canyon edge. Oh, I know what it is. I've just seen it from another place. My family uses it as a target!''

Klyn considered the bare place. It was where he'd emerged from the Keeper land. And it was that place where the horses had moved to avoid the edge!

She was saying, ''I must go back. This has been such a treat. Thank you.''

He looked over at her and smiled. He said, ''The horses have walked. It would be good for them to jog or race a bit.''

She suggested cheerfully, ''I'll take two yards lead, and I'll whistle when I begin to run this horse. Will he run? Or will he idly meander?''

Klyn replied thoughtfully, ''I don't know. I don't race them.''

Elizabeth commented, ''Well, it's time to try! I'll yell when you can start!'' And just like that, she was off with her horse stretched out and barreling along!

Klyn yelled, ''Hey!''

But only her laughter drifted back to him. She gave no starting call. He followed. His horse was loving the run. The horse was closing the gap between them, and soon he'd be alongside her.

Klyn had planned to pass her and tip his Stetson, but he was shocked to see his own arm snake out and lift her from the other horse…so easily! Elizabeth's horse ran on, slowing, looking back and then ahead.

Klyn allowed his horse to slow and the other did also. Elizabeth wiggled and laughed and protested! But he held her…easily…one-armed.

He slowed his horse to a standstill. He didn't allow Elizabeth to stand down on the ground, but pulled her across the front of him and kissed her.

How shocking!

He'd just met her!

Elizabeth looked at him very seriously as she lay in his arms. "You're outrageous."

"I've wanted to kiss you and hold you since I saw you just a couple of hours ago."

Lying dormant across him, with heavy-lidded eyes, she repeated with a sigh, "Outrageous."

He laughed.

"I need to go back to my car."

"Where's that?" He smiled down at her mischievously and waited for her reply.

She asked lazily, "Weren't you paying attention?"

He told her seriously, "I watched you."

"No." She shook her head. "You were

watching all around. Keeping track. Being careful. You made me feel very secure."

He promised right away, "You're safe with us."

"Us?" She looked around.

"These horses are very careful. Do you see your horse? He's waiting for me to give you back to him. He likes having you on his back."

She didn't look at the horse, she watched Klyn. Then she said, "You can let me go now."

Quite softly, Klyn said, "Well, darn."

Elizabeth laughed and shifted so that she could be released and get back on her own horse.

Klyn said, "I'll get down and bring your horse over to you."

"I thought it would be interesting for me to just reach over and remount onto mine...without touching the ground again."

Klyn grinned. "Do you see a difference between the horses? They're twins. How is yours different from this one?"

"I ride him."

Klyn laughed. He pulled her close in a hug. "I like having you close."

"We've only just met."

He looked at his watch. "I've watched you for hours now."

She mentioned, "You watched my chest for an hour or more."

Klyn laughed. "How come you didn't wear some other clothes? You always dress shockingly thataway?"

"Laura called and said for me to get over to her house right then! That I needed to meet this guy who'd come for lunch." She smiled sweetly.

Klyn tilted his head and commented, "So you hurried?" He nodded a couple of times as if he accepted that she had.

He laughed. And as he laughed, he hugged her to him. She was so soft. So very different against his male body. She was a woman. How was he to seal her into his life and keep her?

Elizabeth said, "I must go home. You have lured me away from things I must do. I need to get back home and get things done."

"You're a slave?"

She grinned. "Mostly. My schedule is appalling. But this day has been so special. I rarely get outside and see what all there is to watch. Thank you for this time."

He urged, "Come help me find who is shooting those great silent bullets onto Keeper land."

Elizabeth gasped, "Somebody is shooting at you all?"

"Every once in a while."

"And you have no idea who?"

"None."

With droll humor, she said, "If I stay around you, I'll probably get shot."

Klyn's eyes widened at the idea, the danger. "I take it back. I'll do it."

She misunderstood and thought he was rejecting her help. She said, "I really would like to help. Why can't I?"

"I don't want you hurt."

She laughed. "No one anywhere around here would hurt me. They wouldn't have any reason!"

"If they are shooting at us and our stock, they have reason to be treated as hostile."

She pushed out her lower lip thoughtfully. "I can understand that."

He walked the horse with her on it all the way back to the Whites' house. He never let her go. The other horse followed.

Bob came out of the house as they approached. He frowned. "Is she hurt?"

"Naw," Klyn said, smiling.

Elizabeth just smiled.

Bob laughed, and amazingly, he went back into the house!

By then, Klyn had slid Elizabeth to the ground. She was a little mussed up. She adjusted her clothing…the long-sleeve silk had no need to be adjusted. The black matador's jacket was easily put in place with the selfish safety pins holding it.

Her hair was up under his hat and her cheeks were unusually pinkened. Her eyes danced.

Klyn smiled. He watched Elizabeth. He said, "I find I don't want you to go out with any other man."

She offhandedly replied, "He's completely harmless."

That statement boggled Klyn's basic understanding of women. He gasped. He knew men. He looked off to one side to be sure his ears had heard what she'd actually said!

Klyn had seldom met a man who wasn't dangerous for any woman. A whole lot of them knew how to act, and their control was astonishing. There were, of course, men who did not care for women. But there were men who didn't pay any attention to self-discipline! They either pleaded or they just wrestled the woman on down.

And Elizabeth had said, without any hesitation, that a man was...harmless. A *man?* A man with a *woman?* Klyn looked at Elizabeth again. She appeared stable. She seemed to understand this world.

But she thought a man was harmless. That rocked the boat. And she was talking, so he listened a little late.

"—never occurred to me to just go across the land and look. You've been so kind to escort me around and let me see the area from another perspective. I'd only seen it through the car window from the road. We've never walked down into the canyon. Mother said it isn't safe, and Daddy says it's rotten with bad sand and dangerous animals."

Klyn nodded thoughtfully, considering her background at home, and he said, "I'll teach you to recognize what's good and what's bad."

Elizabeth was delighted! She laughed and briefly flung her arms around his neck. He was startled and only getting his arms up to enclose her when she'd already pulled away, still celebrating that he would take her down into the canyon! She was exuberant!

He was extremely pleased that she was so

glad to search with him. He said, "How'll you get over here to go with me?"

She shrugged in that fascinating way women do and put out her hands as she told him, "I'll just say Tina's computer is stuck, and I need to help her."

Klyn nodded once as he considered how slick she was. His eyes serious, he said, "You're sly."

She took a deep breath and explained, "You must have very easy parents. When you finally meet mine, you'll find they are like guards."

His eyes began to dance and he said, "I just wonder what sort of mama you'll be."

Again, Elizabeth shrugged and replied immediately, "Stringent. We'll just see who rules."

He had to laugh. She was a handful. He wondered how long it would take for her to cotton to him...before he solved the gun problem and left that area.

Elizabeth took off the hat Klyn had loaned her. She folded it exactly as it had been folded in his bag.

He said, "Keep it. You can use it."

She continued to fold the hat as she sassed, "You may find a poor pilgrim who is lost and hatless. This way, you won't have to give him your Stetson.''

Klyn licked his smile and said gently, "I'll remember your kindness.''

"I'll wear my own hat and bring my own horse and find you! You're wonderful company—''

His breathing picked up.

Elizabeth then finished, ''—and I feel safe with you.''

He said in disgust, ''Well, hell.''

She laughed. She blew him a kiss and said, ''I have to tell the Whites goodbye.'' And she ran into the house. Just like that.

Klyn took a careful breath and found he could actually still breathe. He looked around to be sure he would figure out where the hell he was. Then he got on his horse and walked it down the driveway, pulling along the other horse.

Elizabeth was something he needed. He knew he was walking the horses away from her, but it gradually came to him that he was also going in the right direction! How fortunate he was. He wouldn't have to turn around and go back or jump fences to get to town.

Klyn looked at the overcast sky. It would be suppertime when he finally got back to—

The sound of a car whispered in back of him
and the horn tapped once very gently. He'd already moved over to the side of the road.

Elizabeth pulled alongside slowly. She
grinned at him and said, "I called home. Daddy
said it's late in the day for you to try to get back
to town. He thinks you ought to come on over
to our house for supper. It's going to rain."

Klyn told her, "You have a date."

She tilted her head. She grinned. She said, "I
called and said we had company, and I would
be unable to go along with him tonight." She
looked preciously serious, but there were those
wicked eyes that danced and that little smile,
which she licked.

Klyn looked ahead at the almost blocked sun,
and he tilted his Stetson as he said, "I'm
obliged. We could stop on some vacant property
to eat from my bag and spend the night, but
undoubtedly it will rain." He sighed with endurance.

Elizabeth glanced at the clouding sky and
said, "There's probably going to be a shocking
storm. I'm so glad I could find you." Her face
was earnest and very kind.

Sitting astride his patient horse, Klyn eyed the
sky and nodded.

* * *

It was no problem for him to follow her car; she drove very slowly.

Klyn maneuvered his horses so that he was on her side of the car. As she drove along beside him and his interested horses, he told her, "You've done this before?"

She replied, "You would be appalled!" She grinned at him.

So Klyn asked Elizabeth, "How many times and for who all?"

She sighed hugely and replied, "Daddy. He will never just come on in for lunch or supper. He's a very difficult m-m-m-m—person."

Klyn asked, "What were all the '*m*'s about?"

"Men."

He grinned at her. "You got trouble with men?"

"I'd never known that. It can't be every man who's stubborn."

"I didn't even argue about us going to your house." And his face was just as open and innocent as a newborn babe!

She laughed.

It was interesting how slowly she could drive the car alongside his walking horse. Klyn and Elizabeth talked and laughed quite a bit. Anybody watching the two strangers would have thought they'd known each other for a long old time, they had so much to say.

The only problem was along the highway. Elizabeth drove moderately along the road, while Klyn galloped his horses carefully along in the shadows of the late afternoon.

When they got to the Moores' lane, they eased along more slowly.

They arrived at Elizabeth's house, and she called in that she'd brought their guest.

Before they went into the house, Elizabeth found Klyn a place where the horses would be safe, and he gave them water and feed.

Once he'd finished tending the horses, he told Elizabeth he would be right back. He walked off a way and brushed off his clothing and Stetson.

Klyn came back to her and said, "You can kiss me now."

She grinned and replied, "Both of my parents are in the upstairs room, looking around the mesquite to see what on earth we're doing."

So Klyn promised, "I'll save the kiss until later."

Elizabeth laughed softly and licked her lips as she said, "How thoughtful."

In the house, Elizabeth told her parents how

she'd spent part of the afternoon with Klyn and had seen the wonderful area in the canyon.

Her daddy said, "It's been there a long time."

Klyn mentioned, "We Keepers've been in this area for quite a while."

Mr. Moore said, "My family came here from the low East Coast after the War of Secession."

Elizabeth asked Klyn, "How long have your folks been around?"

Rather than tromp on Mr. Moore's toes, Klyn just said, "A long, long old time."

Both parents saw that Klyn had good manners. He was a gentleman. Why was he there? they wondered.

So they asked.

And Klyn told about Andrew invading the Keepers' fence and his horse being shot. Then about Tom Keeper whose horse was panicked by a silent bullet. And he told about the animals whose bones showed bullets.

Mr. Moore said, "There's a whole lot of people around these parts who shoot into the canyon and along the river."

Klyn replied, "I'm trying to find out if any of them fire large, silent bullets that travel a long distance, not far off the ground."

Mrs. Moore said, "I'll help you find out."

Klyn lifted a hand and said earnestly, "I appreciate that. But you're a citizen here. You have to be careful for your family. Don't get involved. Leave it to the sheriff and me. It's his job, and it's my family."

Mr. Moore commented, "Those Keepers are good folks. They've been here a long old time. I'd like to help them."

Klyn said very kindly, "Thank you. But not this time. It could possibly be too dangerous for you all."

Elizabeth's daddy turned his head a trifle as if to listen more intently. "Too...dangerous?"

How like a man to pick up a verbal gauntlet off the floor.

Klyn licked his smile as his eyes danced in delight. But his controlled reply was careful. "You're a man. You don't want to be left out of anything. But this time, please be careful for your family's sake. However, if you hear of any activity that is...different, please call the sheriff. That would be a big help to us."

Mr. Moore said, "I'll watch."

Klyn replied, "Thank you."

Four

As the women worked in the kitchen to prepare dinner, Mr. Moore said to Klyn, "You know, I seriously doubt anybody around here would fire such a silent gun as you've mentioned. I've never even heard tell of one shooting over onto Keeper land."

Klyn replied kindly, "It could be that they don't realize the bullet goes so far. And they could be missing the cliff face on the other side of the canyon. When we looked at that area today, your bright daughter was the one who made me think about that naked portion at the top.

"Back when I was on the other side of the canyon, I was looking for a place to get down into the river area and up the other side. At that particular bare place at the top of the cliff was where the horses moved aside and walked farther in from the edge."

"Ahhhh," Mr. Moore said. "Now I understand their problem. Some person with a humongous firing piece shoots at the cliff, sometimes missing the cliff, and the silent bullet goes farther east onto Keeper land."

Klyn nodded to indicate that Mr. Moore had hit the nail on its head. "Just think of all the people who waste bullets on the area, and *some* of the bullets cause problems on over a way. It's dangerous. We haven't yet lost a man, but the Keeper now in hospital was close. We need to know how to stop this silent bullet."

Mr. Moore asked, "How do we find out?"

But Klyn shook his head. "You all need to back off from that. Like I've said, just leave it to me and the sheriff. We'll find out."

Mr. Moore then said, "How about a column in the local paper? If somebody is being careless, we need to mention how."

Klyn nodded in agreement and said, "I'll talk to the sheriff."

Mrs. Moore came in, lifted her eyebrows at her husband, and that signaled the end of the intense discussion.

The Moores had a room available that belonged to a son who was at college. They invited Klyn to stay the night.

Before turning in, Klyn went out to settle the horses for the night. Elizabeth came out after Klyn to stand and watch.

The corral was a place that hadn't been used in some time. So it was especially clean and the grasses were freshly cut and stacked. The Moores took good care of their place.

Everyone was ready for bed relatively early. Even Klyn found that his eyes drooped.

After they'd all said good-night to each other, they went to their rooms, and the night was quickly silent.

After a perfect shower, Klyn's body was clean and smelled good. His hair was washed.

Naked, he got into bed and realized he was very tired. His thoughts kept going to who was responsible for the shockingly silent bullets. Who could be the villain? Who could do such a dumb thing?

Thinking then of Elizabeth, he wondered

when she would come to him. He turned over to look at her brother's clock. It was still early. She was waiting for her parents to fall asleep, he figured.

He waited. He listened to the splats of big raindrops. So *that* was why she and her parents had allowed him to sleep inside their house! They knew it was going to rain!

But maybe, just maybe, Elizabeth still might slide quietly into his room. It would be so nice to have her under that light blanket.

His body would fire up—just like that—and he'd want to get rid of the blanket! She'd gasp and whisper, and he'd kiss her and make her forget she'd ever been cold. Yeah.

He smiled in the darkness and thought about her sliding naked into his bed. He got up and sprinkled even more aftershave on his face…under his arms…along his neck.

As time ticked away, Klyn wondered if Elizabeth was actually coming to his room. Her *brother's* room. Would that wobble her? Their making love on her brother's bed?

He slid back into bed, breathing a little too fast. That would rattle her if he went on breathing thataway. He practiced breathing slower. Calmer.

And he went to sleep.

* * *

When Klyn wakened, he sagged in disappointment. His sex was still eager from all the wild dreams he'd had during the night.

He got out of the bed and dressed. Then he stripped the bed and carried the bedding to the laundry room.

In the kitchen, the entire Moore family shared a seriously large breakfast with easy banter and casual talk.

Klyn looked at Elizabeth who was busy with breakfast. Her sisters were laughing and teasing.

Elizabeth saw that Klyn watched her. She smiled at him as she busily helped her mother. The breakfast was superb, but Klyn couldn't help wondering why she hadn't come to his bed. *That* was what he'd wanted! Not this remarkable food!

Klyn was sober-faced and pretended to listen…enough…as the family all talked.

He at least knew the subject was intrusion on their lands this side of the river. It was people hunting. It wasn't silent bullets. It was noisy dogs and men and even women who carried flasks of spirits.

He nodded. How could he do anything else?

When breakfast was finished, Klyn allowed
Elizabeth to go out to the barn with him. There,
Klyn watched Elizabeth seriously, and he found
she wasn't grieving that he was leaving! She was
sleepy, but being very courteous. Well, she'd
just met him the day before.

He saddled the horses and repacked his gear.
And part of the packing was the food Mrs.
Moore had pushed onto Klyn. He licked his
smile.

So after promising to keep in touch with Elizabeth, Klyn mounted one horse and told the
other horse they were leaving.

Then he again said goodbye to Elizabeth before he rode away. She stood for a long time,
watching him leave. He turned several times and
just looked back at her. She was still there.

When Klyn entered town, he went to the sheriff's office. Bob White was not there. Klyn had
some idea as to all the things that happened in
such an area and how often the sheriff had to go
see what the hell else was taking place.

Anybody would think such a small number of
people spread out thataway would be easy for a
sheriff to handle. It wasn't so. People quarreled

over the dumbest things! Land, horses, cattle. Women. Even wives! And on occasion—men!

But now the sheriff had to cope with that bullet fired from their area across Keeper land. If it wasn't one thing, it was ten others. Being a sheriff and keeping the peace was a hell of a job.

Klyn went over to his hotel room and called his family. He asked, ''You all know of any more bullets? Anything hurt? Is someone still shooting onto Keeper land?''

No one knew of any such thing.

Klyn's cousin Tom said, ''Not that we know of these last couple of weeks. Not since my horse was panicked. But we've avoided standing in the crossfire area.''

Klyn said drollfully into the phone, ''Well, I can understand that.''

Tom asked with interest. ''What all have you found out?''

Klyn replied, ''On the east side of the canyon there's a blank place where nothing grows on its face. I saw it. There are scrawny trees above it. And I found that particular position is used as a target for shooting across the river from the opposite side of the canyon.''

Tom said softly, "I've not questioned that any time along the way! Dumb!"

Klyn replied easily, "I wouldn't have even wondered, since the place is Keeper property and none of us comes over this way very often. A female gave me the basics when she wondered if the outside of the cliff had fallen for some reason."

"Wow."

"Yep. A woman."

Tom said, "Be careful."

Klyn commented, "It isn't the woman shooting rifles that sends silent bullets onto Keeper land."

"It could be."

Klyn replied, "Yeah. I guess you're right. But how would a woman hold such a potent gun?"

Tom asked softly, "Maybe it's two of them?"

"I used to think it was women who were sly, but there are a whole bunch of sly men."

"Yeah."

Klyn admitted, "I'm growing up."

"Welcome to the crowd."

Klyn laughed without humor.

The very next day, Klyn Keeper got to the sheriff's office and Bob White was there.

The sheriff said, "So, you're still here."

Klyn grinned. He tilted his Stetson back and sat down on one of the chairs as he agreed, "Still here."

The sheriff told Klyn, "I'm still trying to figure out who's doing this. I've checked and the regular bullets don't go farther than the canyon face."

Klyn mused, "That canyon face is something that has interested me. That's the bull's-eye for all the shooters around here?"

"Mostly. We know it's been used thataway for many generations."

Klyn mentioned, "All us Keepers appreciate the work you've done for us. You're a good man."

Bob White frowned. "I don't feel like a good man. I'm flustered and irritated and find the whole thing obnoxious because I can't wave a hand and finish it."

"I know."

"Everybody around here thinks good of Keepers, who've been tolerant and kind to us all. It would seem that we could find whoever is firing those silent bullets down that area of the Keeper place."

"Yes."

The sheriff went on, "I don't know what else to do. The bullets come from somewheres, but we can't find out where. And this has gone on for some long time."

"I know."

"Why do those one kind of bullets go so far?"

Klyn shrugged and added, "Why are they so silent?"

"Yeah." Bob White sat back and pulled on his lower lip as he looked blankly out the window.

Klyn said kindly, "I'll be around. Let me know if you find some brilliant idea about all this."

"Yeah." But it was a positive response to nothing.

Even Klyn understood that. He got up and resettled his Stetson. He said, "Take care of yourself."

"Yeah." Looking out the window, not seeing even that, the sheriff didn't move.

So Klyn left. He went out quietly, thinking they would never find out who was the culprit of the silent shootings. It would continue and more of the Keeper animals would be killed. Or they'd be wounded in such a way that they'd have to be killed. Or it could be people who were hit next time.

The last thought bolstered Klyn's determination.

Klyn rode his horse over to the Moores' house, the other horse following along.

Arriving there, in that glorious TEXAS weather, Klyn breathed deeply and smiled. He slid off his horse and told the two horses to behave as he tied them to a fence.

Elizabeth opened the front door, and she looked delightedly surprised and welcoming. She made it seem as though she was the first to respond to his knock. Actually, it had been her mother whom Elizabeth stopped dead in her tracks. Elizabeth had smiled and put a finger to her lips to silence her mother. She told her mama, "The horses are tied in our road."

Mrs. Moore gasped, then she thought if this couple did marry, then she and her husband could get rid of it all!

Mrs. Moore watched as her daughter opened the door and the two young people smiled at each other. Elizabeth appeared surprised to find him there. As if she hadn't known.

Elizabeth opened the door wider.

Klyn grinned at her.

Elizabeth exclaimed, "Why, how nice!"

Klyn's smile was wide. And he began to remove his Stetson.

Elizabeth said, "You've been brilliant with the horses."

Klyn licked his grin and nodded.

"We could ride off a distance and...be alone." She had on trousers. Riding would be easy.

He gasped. "What an innovative idea!"

Elizabeth laughed. Being a thoughtful child, she called to her now absent mother, "We'll be back in a while."

Her mother called, "You finish the wash!"

But Elizabeth left the house with Klyn. With his help, she got on one of the horses. Obviously she hadn't heard her mother.

The two on horseback went on off and away.

She wobbled Klyn.

They rode slowly and talked and laughed. They acted as if they weren't in any hurry at all.

Elizabeth waved at people who labored on the highway and called back comments. She didn't ever stop because she hadn't locked Klyn in yet

and she didn't want any female thief stealing her
man away.

Her eyes twinkled.

Klyn glanced off in a thinking manner and
said, "I'm not *entirely* wobbled over you. I happen to like you and I'm...about to go crazy with
you around here so isolated. Is that okay with
you?"

She laughed.

He told her, "I have an interesting meet today. I'll tell you about it later."

She nodded and said, "Okay."

So they took the horses onto a side street of
the town and talked as they rode along.

In a town that little, the people were aware of
everything. As the two rode along on Klyn's
horses, the neighbors came out on their porches
and waved as they called out greetings.

The two waved back, but they seldom called
out anything vocal. They just laughed.

Klyn told her, "You're beautiful. No woman
I've ever known could hold a candle to you."

And she said, "Oh? How many women do
you know?"

So he told her, "I move around a whole lot
of places."

She lifted her eyebrows. "You're

not...employed?'' She watched him with rather intent interest.

Klyn's attention was caught and he licked his lips as he said openly, ''This thing about the strange bullets on Keeper land is very serious. I'm trying to help my relatives who own the land on beyond, east of the river.''

She asked carefully, ''You don't own the Keeper land?''

He shook his head. ''Not a square acre.''

That made her a tad indignant. ''What about the women who are Keepers?''

Klyn looked off as men tend to do and he replied, ''Women rarely buy any land on their own.''

''Oh.''

Klyn looked over at Elizabeth and asked, ''What's the 'oh' mean?''

She shrugged her shoulders in a way that lifted her shirt over her breasts very interestingly. She told Klyn, ''I thought you owned the Keeper land.''

He gasped and put a hand to his chest rather dramatically as he said, ''Heavens to Betsy, no! Not me. The land just across the river all belongs now to my cousin, Tom Keeper.''

She slid her head around slowly as she looked at Klyn. "Isn't *your* last name Keeper?"

Klyn licked a rampant smile as he replied, "My name's Keeper, but the portion across the river here belongs to Tom Keeper. Just their name is a clue. They keep what they have." He grinned as he underlined that.

She considered him soberly, then looked away from Klyn. She licked her lips, knowing full well that she had his attention, and sighed.

He adjusted his hat and said, "Wait a minute. What are you thinking?"

"Nothing." She looked around and then said, "I believe I'll just go on home."

With a very blank face, Klyn said, "I thought you wanted to be with me. What's the matter?"

Elizabeth gave him a very kind look. She said, "I thought you owned that land over yonder."

He cleared his throat to cover his laugh. He told her, "No. I'm just a taggle end of the Keepers."

She was caught by his earnestness. She looked at him clearly. He was exceptional even if he was poor. She smiled at him.

He grinned and said, "You've been very kind to me. I appreciate that."

She replied, "You're a nice person."

Klyn was silent as they rode on his horses
down the town's streets. They didn't say anything to each other. It was as if they'd finished?
The bottom of the bucket was empty? Were they
comfortable as silent people? Did they just not
have anything else to comment about? Or was
she aware now that he was a poor man who had
no land?

Klyn took Elizabeth back toward her house.
Along the way, she'd waved to just about every
citizen in that small town.

He inquired, "You gonna run for Congress?"

She looked at him and frowned in some con-
fusion.

He gestured with one hand as he said, "Everybody knows you. And you wave back like
some politician that's won the voters."

"I hadn't thought of doing that. By golly, I'd
be in the State House!"

He tilted his head thoughtfully and replied, "I
was thinking about D.C."

"Why, I might do that! Thanks for the idea."
And her whole attitude changed. She sat
straighter. She waved differently. Not with such
enthusiasm. She smiled a tad and nodded her
head rather formally.

Klyn was so amused. He said, "You could soothe your most ardent voter."

"Oh." She considered. "I can never thank you enough for this idea. You are brilliant. I've never thought of doing something so intense!"

He suggested, "Let's go over to the empty barn."

She laughed and blushed as she shook her head.

He teased her. "I'm pure. You ought to train me on how to be with women."

She suggested, "Learning about people might change my attitude."

"Change...your...attitude?" He frowned trying to figure it out.

"In D.C."

"Brilliant."

She pushed her hair back and said, "It's something to consider."

So he said, "Would it be okay if I wrote a book about your adventure?"

Elizabeth shrugged her shoulders. She said kindly, "By the time you'd written the book, I'd be experienced in politics enough, and you'd make a fortune."

He laughed as he always did with Elizabeth, and with increasing certainty he knew that he was falling for this special lady.

Five

Klyn was due at a meeting not too long ahead. He looked at his watch and considered. Then he looked around at the area. He wished he had his dog there. Who knew who might turn up?

Nudging Klyn's attention, Elizabeth said in a very offhanded way, "Don't get used to me. I might find somebody that I can marry."

Klyn agreed with the budding woman. "Without question. I see the guys watch you." He was surprised, then, to hear his own, older, more sophisticated voice saying, "I'd want to view the man who wants you to be sure he is worthwhile.''

Looking off as if bored, Elizabeth had the audacity to say, ''How would you know?''

Carefully, Klyn commented, ''If you'll see to it that I get to check out the man, you'd be safe.''

Elizabeth commented, ''How would you know 'safe' even if you saw it?''

Klyn replied quite logically, ''I know women and what they need in men.''

Elizabeth said easily and with no emphasis at all, ''That must boggle you.''

Shock did boggle him then. But he finally just replied, ''I know.'' Klyn said that with a rather dramatic sigh. He was good at drama. But then, he'd been in plays all through school.

Elizabeth said thoughtfully, ''I'd like the man a little taller than you so—''

''Taller!'' His gasp was indignant.

Trying to seem cool, Elizabeth continued, ''I need a man a couple of inches taller so that I could easily wear heels.''

''I'm *taller* than you even when you're wearing heels!''

She only smiled kindly. Still unmoved, she

replied gently, "Yes, but the man I would want would be just a tad taller."

What man could she find who was better than he? Klyn snarled, "He'd break his neck trying to hug you against his body as he kisses you."

Looking around, Elizabeth told Klyn, "If he's tall enough, he will have figured out how to do that."

Klyn was really shocked. He moved his head so that he looked at that woman's face. She was gorgeous.

What she wanted was a man to marry. He ought to back off a little more and let her search out the man.

A male cousin of his had told him, "You'll have a really rough time of it until you get married. You're a Keeper. You'll have responsibilities. You'll be sought after by people who need help. You'll have to find a good wife."

The first time Klyn heard that, he'd laughed.

But this time he was spending with Elizabeth was getting more and more serious. What if this budding woman should find another man? Could he find another woman who was even similar to her? Ahhh, that was the problem. He was too young at twenty-seven to be married. Wasn't he?

Should he go on looking? This female was

alluring, but she might well get sloppy and smoke cigars. She could let the house get tacky as she read paperbacks. Who knew?

At twenty-seven, he was too young to commit to marriage. How could he keep her otherwise? Actually, at his age, he was old enough. He was unsettled. He wasn't ready to be serious about any single woman. He had time to taste women and see what the difference was. Didn't he?

She sighed.

He asked, "You okay?"

She replied softly and dragged the two words out long enough when she said, "I suppose."

Next to her on his horse, he was shivering with need and he was probably dripping scalding sweat. His breathing was not normal. He said, "I probably…want…you." That wasn't at all eager, but he did get the words out.

She tilted her head and looked off to the side. She said, "Balderdash."

He lifted his shocked head so that he could look at her face. "What'd you say?"

In a bored manner, she mentioned, "You need to practice kisses."

That made him indignant. *"What!"*

"You probably try hard, but you need some

guidance. Being a woman, I can only tell you how to practice.''

Klyn was stunned. He was indignant. He was amused. He was just about ready to leave for the meeting that the sneaked glimpse at his watch alerted him had already started.

Her attitude was not eager. Was she…teasing him? Tempting him? Or was she making him feel potentially discarded so that he'd work hard to get her?

That was interesting. He waited for her to say something to him. He knew he was perfect. So to prove himself, he reached across to her on the other horse and put his big hand on her shoulder as he asked, ''You okay?''

''Ummmmmm.''

He watched her with some odd interest and said, ''Yeah.'' That's what men say when they don't know exactly what else to say to a woman. In those circumstances, talking doesn't always get a man anywhere. Klyn said, ''Do you know there's a cat right over there watching us?''

''Where?''

Klyn watched the budding woman as he said, ''Right over there. Do you suppose he's learning how to meet with a female?''

Elizabeth scoffed, ''It *is* a female.''

Never taking his eyes from her, he asked, "How do you know?"

Elizabeth moved her hand. "She's three colors."

"I thought the cat looked young...and uninterested."

Elizabeth asked, "Why do males assume they are the ones who are watched?"

So he said, "Why are you insulted that it isn't you who is watched?"

She sighed as she again explained with some patience, "The cat is female."

Klyn was really a little annoyed by her.

She laughed.

He told her, "I have an appointment. Do you need my help getting home? The time passed quicker than I thought. You're distracting."

She watched him with some curiosity, then said, "No."

"I need to go on." Being a gentleman, he added, "I'll be in touch." He smiled. Oh, hell. He couldn't leave her there alone. He reminded her, "You shouldn't stay here by yourself."

She said, "How kind you are." She was being snide.

Calmly he told her, "I'll be late. May I help

you home? Or can you ride my horse there, and I'll pick it up later?''

Elizabeth looked aloofly at him for a minute before she said, ''I find I'm being discarded.''

He laughed softly. What else could he do with the time so short? ''I need to speak to the men at the meeting. I need to tell them about the canyon.''

''Yes.'' She was waiting for him to leave. She was using his extra horse. She'd been alone all over that area. And she'd been safe. The people around were aware and watched.

Klyn had moved his horse away a tad. He told Elizabeth, ''You're a very interesting woman.''

She chuckled.

Klyn told her, ''I've seen it today. Is it something you generally hide?''

She shrugged her shoulders.

He told her yet again, ''I'm looking for whoever it is that sends a bullet through the Keeper land.''

She delayed him a tad longer by saying, ''You don't care if the person harms this area?''

''He hasn't as yet.''

''Why would he harm the Keeper land?''

Restless, aware he was already late, Klyn told

her, "You need to get out of this area. It's too isolated for a woman to be in it alone."

"I will."

"I can't stay. The men are meeting right now. I need to get there and talk to them about the silent bullets."

Elizabeth looked at him for a minute before she said, "You need to hurry."

He replied, "I no longer have time to see you home. I'm already late. Allow me to help you get on your way back to your house."

She walked the horse past him. She told him, "I've ridden here a hundred times." She had the sass to tell him, "I'll be in touch."

He watched her as he licked his smile.

She knew he was anxious for his meeting.

Sometimes one learns something *not* to do at an odd encounter. An odd place. It had been a serious foolishness. She had learned her mistake. And she had no immediate time to smooth it out. He was already late. He needed her out of that place and on his horse. Then he could hurry to the meeting.

She turned around and watched him leave her. He did not look back.

Elizabeth was very serious. She didn't ride the horse, she was just on his back. She allowed the horse to go as he pleased. She only suggested where with the reins.

She'd thought with a man like Klyn, she could be sassy, and he would be entertained. He had seemed so. He was not.

She considered what she might do to help him see her differently.

She wondered if he'd be interested enough to come back to get his horse—and to see her.

Klyn probably had no reason to come back. More than likely, he had other things to do throughout the area that were more interesting to him than she had been.

Elizabeth was thoughtful. Klyn had been very kind to her. She would talk to him when he came for his horse.

Riding like a madman, Klyn reached the small town. He slid off his horse under a small tree, then loosened the saddle binder and took the horse to a trough for water. He put the horse on a line with a snap of its tether. Then he went into the meeting hall just as the gathering was about finished.

Klyn walked to the head of the meeting and nodded to those men in charge.

They looked at him soberly.

He smiled and said, "I got lost."

They blinked and then they laughed. "We'll git cha a map."

Klyn looked at the older men who watched him with dead eyes. They had dismissed him.

Klyn smiled at them just a tad and said, "I beg your pardons."

Then he had the audacity to go right into the question of the big gun, which was shooting far over into Keeper land. He was so skilled in his comments that the gathered men stayed and paid close attention.

They not only heard all about the odd gun that fired far over Keeper land, they watched a good man tell of it. They listened carefully to what Klyn had to say. He was earnest, knowledgeable and he could say what they needed to hear in order to watch and help.

At the end of Klyn's speech, the men decided among themselves to keep this young stranger in their territory and to run him for the House. They needed an articulate man who knew what he was talking about because they had a few other problems besides the silent bullets.

So when he was finished talking, they gathered around him and asked Klyn other questions.

The young Keeper was astonishingly cognizant. Only the other, younger men who weren't allowed much talk could appreciate the fact that the older men not only understood Klyn, they *listened!*

That one of their ilk could manage to make the older men just listen was very invigorating.

The younger men not only listened but they watched the older men with some pride that they'd finally found a voice they would take in. It was simply astonishing that the older men respected someone who was younger than their own age. It was a miracle. And the younger men looked at Klyn differently.

So it was that when the older men reluctantly started to leave, the younger men caught up with Klyn Keeper and said, "We gotta talk to you."

Klyn lifted his head as he listened to those sparse words. He had no knowledge of the young men, but he did remember that he'd been with one of their females for a time that very day. The young men could gang up on him and tear him apart. He said, "Why." No question. Just the opening to know what they wanted.

In variations, the young men said, "It's about you staying around."

Klyn grinned. "I thought you had me confused with some careless man who was luring a sister.''

The young guys laughed. Then they said, ''Tell us about the bullets. Tell us what you know so far.''

Even Klyn knew how curious young men are about something that isn't clear. They're the ones who like adventure. They're the ones who are not risk-free.

So Klyn said, ''For some long years, we've had problems with a large, silent bullet coming onto Keeper land. Keepers have come over here, and they've watched and listened, but none of them discovered why or when or from where that bullet comes. If *any* of you suspect anyone around here, let's find out who it might be.''

The young ones all nodded, but not at once. Each one assimilated the problem differently.

One asked, ''Have you watched?''

Klyn nodded. ''We've found the shot is at odd times and not at all often. We get to the point where we believe it is finished, but then it happens again. That's what put a cousin of mine in hospital. He was riding a horse who heard the whistle of something and tried to get out of the way, but he pitched my cousin. The horse wasn't hurt, but he was grazed across the chest.''

One man nodded. "I've heard about that."

Another commented, "Probably all of us have heard about the bullets. We watch. Whatever gun it is, it's a damned big silent one."

That reply especially caught the attention of Klyn. He hadn't realized how interested the people there were about the strange silent bullet that had been boggling the Keepers across the river and beyond the cliffs.

One asked seriously, "I hear you've been around this area a time. That woman you watching or funning?"

Klyn asked, "Who was that?"

The dumped man said quietly, "Her name's Betty May."

Klyn shook his head and said quietly, "I don't know her. Could you have made a mistake and said the wrong thing to her?"

The young man's face was serious. He replied, "I don't think so."

So Klyn said very gently to just that young man, "Take her some flowers and remember to remove your hat, but don't stay long and don't try anything. Hear?"

The guy grinned. "I'll be good."

Klyn smiled. "Good luck."

The young man replied, "I'll probably need that."

"Be careful with her."

And the young man promised with a smile, "I will."

Klyn turned his head once and said, "I mean, don't take her, just give her the flowers and listen to her."

The rejected man blinked a couple of times and replied, "Okay. I can do that."

Some other young guy came closer and asked, "What're you talking about?"

Klyn said, "Women."

That, oddly enough, brought over more of the young men. They listened and watched, their heads turning to whoever was talking.

The curious one's eyes slid over to the younger man and he said, "You been talking about my girl?"

The young man said, "We'll see if she is."

But the other man said, "Back off."

And the young man promised, "It's not what you think. It's something else entirely. I just got help in smoothing a relationship.

So the other man asked Klyn, "You giving out advice?"

Klyn replied, "I wish I had that moxie."

"You...ain't?"

And Klyn shook his head as he grinned. "I'm nothing any woman swoons over."

That made them all laugh.

So the young men continued to talk. They talked about the bullet that whizzed over the land. They exchanged things they'd seen or heard.

It was a time of real help for Klyn.

Finally, they went their various ways. They called to one another where they would be going.

Alone, Klyn mused how strange the response of the young men had been. He had been talked down to for so long, it was surprising for him to be considered a leader. Even the older men had watched him and listened to him.

These men wanted him as their leader. They had found the bullets shot so far onto Keeper land as wrong. They wanted to help. While the older men wanted to find out why someone did such a thing, the younger men meant to catch the person.

To Klyn, it was very touching to watch the younger men so earnest and willing to catch the person who was shooting those bullets over

Keeper land. Klyn was grateful that he'd come to that area.

That evening, Klyn called his dad and told him all that had happened. His dad said, "Yeah."

Klyn told his dad, "I could be here a while."

His dad said, "Take your time and watch. Don't get involved in any danger to yourself. You have kin who love you and who will come immediately if you need us. Understand?"

Klyn's eyes moistened and he grinned into the phone. "Yes, sir."

"We'll be around here. Call if you need us. Should some of your brothers and cousins come now?"

"Not yet."

"It might be better if some of them were there to listen and watch."

"And everybody would know why they were here, and a real donnybrook would blow."

"Yeah." His dad laughed.

Klyn told his dad, "I'll be in touch."

"Why do I find that I've lost control over you and you're smart enough to handle things by yourself?"

Klyn replied, "You're slow figuring that out. I've been independent since I was twelve."

"At twelve, I *thought* you'd matured, but at that time you still talked child to your mother."

"She's young."

That made Papa Keeper huff, "I'm *not?*"

Klyn only laughed and hung up the phone very gently.

Six

When Klyn Keeper hung up the phone after talking to his dad, he sat for a while just thinking. Did a man who was twenty-seven still have to keep a link to his family? Yeah.

Klyn thought how often he'd used his dad as a sounding board when he'd wanted to do something. His dad had listened. The interesting part was when his dad asked *him*, "What do you think is right?"

Mostly, Klyn had done it all *his* way. His dad made him think, and Klyn had chosen in his own way…after listening to his dad. He couldn't re-

member once that his dad had—well, there'd
been one time when his dad had said, "Think
about it tonight and call me tomorrow."

Klyn sat there with his hand still on the phone,
but his thoughts, as always, drifted to Elizabeth.
When he'd gone to the Moores to retrieve his
horses, Elizabeth hadn't been home. And he really needed to see her again.

So the next day, Klyn called Elizabeth. He
knew he should not. Men really don't have much
self-control. But the phone just rang. Well, he
would mention that to her if she ever spoke to
him again.

He went to the sheriff's office, but the sheriff
wasn't there. His secretary was a little older than
Klyn, and she smiled at him with sparkling eyes.
He reached to touch the brim of his hat in a
gentleman's way and carefully returned her
smile, then left.

It was late afternoon when Klyn walked along
the street and found the corner used as a cross-
road by the young men. He slowed and looked
for anyone he could remember from yesterday's
gathering. Several of the men smiled and greeted
Klyn. They asked, "How come you're free and
watching?"

Klyn bit his grin and just settled his Stetson the way some men do.

That gave them all the opening to tease and taunt.

Klyn laughed. Not only were the men funny, but they were paying attention. A couple of them named those who were talking. The willing guide would say, "Now, Ambrose, you know better than that." Or he would say, "Why, Jimmy, how'd you ever find that out?"

Gradually, Klyn matched names with faces.

The one named Jimmy said in a hushed voice, "Here comes a woman."

They all grinned and lifted their Stetsons a tad. They laughed as she came closer and hats were entirely removed.

Her cheeks were pink. She was shy. All the men walked after her and asked if she'd like to go to a movie or a bar or just fool around?

Getting pinker, she said nothing but shook her head and just walked along.

The guys called goodbyes and whistled and lifted their Stetsons.

Leaning against the street sign's pole, waiting for the guys to come back, Klyn told them, "You boys have got to grow up and be less intrusive."

The guys doubled over, laughing, and denied ever being the least bit "intrusive" on the street in any way.

Klyn waited and smiled gently. Then he said, "If you want a woman for yourself, be earnest and open and very, very careful."

The one named Pete said in shock, "My daddy said that!"

Klyn cautioned him, "Listen to him."

Jimmy gasped, "Parents know about women?"

They all laughed.

Then, with the group's attention, Klyn told them about the strange and dangerous bullet that flew over the canyon far onto Keeper territory.

The one called Sam asked, "How often?"

Klyn replied honestly, "Very seldom. But Keepers have found the big, long, skinny bullets in the bones of buzzard-eaten cattle. No bullets have hit any man that we know. No skeletons. But it did hit a horse who collapsed dead on the pilgrim who'd cut our fence."

Another man, Fuquay, nodded with the others but said, "Too bad *he* wasn't hit."

Klyn replied, "The pilgrim's leg was trapped under the dead horse for several days."

Sam asked, "Who found him?"

Klyn told the whole story in several sentences. He was getting skilled. He ended with "My aunt who is married to John Keeper is a pushover. She believes *everyone* can be good. She could be right. She changed that intruder. You would never believe how much. He is a new man."

Just that comment changed all those around Klyn. How strange. In the years to come, those listeners found a couple of males who didn't *want* to be changed. One left entirely and was never heard from again. The other…changed.

Klyn went from the male group to a female group, asking people to watch and listen and let him know if a big gun was fired.

Since the bullets had never hit their area but only deep into Keeper land, quite a few asked if there was a feud.

Klyn smiled and replied, "We're harmless." And when their chuckle was finished, Klyn said kindly, "Since our land comes to the canyon, no one can claim that we've gobbled up any of their land. Only the river took land in that area."

One of the listeners said, "You all were lucky to get that land."

Klyn mentioned, "It was over five hundred years ago, and it hasn't been easy to keep the Keeper land." He grinned at his word usage. It was something Keepers had used for a long old time. Klyn said, "Don't get involved. Just watch and tell us if you see anything. Here's our phone number. Please and thank you."

Those there all agreed. They nodded or said, "Sure" or "Yeah." One asked, "If you're not at the hotel but have gone home, who do we call?"

"John Keeper. Here's his card with his phone number. He and his son Tom are the owners of that particular Keeper place where those bullets are plowing through. They are uncle and cousin to me."

One of the men said, "You're good to do this for them."

Klyn smiled. "Tom is in hospital because of the bullet which startled his horse who threw him. Coming to this place was an adventure for me. I get to see the area and talk to you all."

His listeners could see that. And they talked about adventures of their own. Most of the adventures had been flops and boring; they had run out of food or water or the horses had gone lame or it rained.

They laughed and bent over and forgot to move to let people walk past. But in a town like that, with so small a number of people, they mostly got more listeners who talked about their own adventures.

Gradually, Klyn noticed that everybody knew who he was. And they *all* knew he knew Elizabeth.

They all thought she was just perfect and calm.

So who did Klyn see walking down the street with a cover of like females who were charmingly pink-cheeked and laughing? Elizabeth Moore.

Klyn watched only her. She carefully ignored him. She stopped and talked to all the guys around who spoke to her, but she ignored Klyn.

His eyes danced and he licked his smile. He said softly just to her, "You haven't asked if I made it to the meeting."

She looked at him and asked quite formally, "And did you get there in time?"

Then she turned her back and tilted her head to listen to another young male.

A CHALLENGE. With caps.

He said to her back through thin lips, "I did make it. By the skin of my teeth. The older men stayed to listen, too, and I met a whole lot of people who were very courteous."

Not looking at him at all, Elizabeth said, "How nice."

Klyn told her kindly, "The younger men stayed and talked and listened. They mostly talked."

She turned her head and looked at him. She looked beyond him and lifted her eyebrows. "They overrode your comments?"

Klyn laughed softly, and his eyes twinkled.

She'd read about "twinkling eyes" and she looked at him intently. His eyes did. How outrageous for a man to snare that perfect gift. She looked away, beyond him and waited for him to soothe her.

He reminded her, "I'm searching for a particular male person." His tone was confidential. He knew no woman was involved—why frighten one?

Elizabeth looked at him and listened.

The other budding ladies who were with her were laughing and protesting the teasing of the males who were delighted the women were there and that they could talk to them. If it hadn't been for having Klyn there, the women would have walked on past. But that Klyn Keeper had drawn Elizabeth like a magnet pulls on iron.

The other females didn't have to chide the

men's talk. The men were careful and courteous. They were trying to get the young women to go with them to a dance that night. The females were careful. They said, "We'll see."

The guys asked, "You waiting to see if anybody else'll ask you?"

But the young women were careful. They needed to know if their parents would okay any one of these sidewalk hooligans. None had any particular good conduct attributed to them.

Klyn was surprised the young women didn't ask the guys to go along to the dance that evening. He said to the young ladies, "Can we dance with you tonight?"

He didn't know if any of the guys had enough money to get somebody *else* into the dance, so he'd just said that.

The ladies looked at each other and raised their eyebrows. They smiled. They laughed. They said, "We'll see."

One of the guys said sadly, "I don't have enough push on me to go if you don't get there. You wouldn't stand me up, would you?"

The young woman said, "I'll be there. I'll save you a dance. Okay?"

He grinned and replied, "Done!"

The other women said that they would also be

there. And the young men said they would go to the dance, too.

Klyn said to Elizabeth, "You gotta go, too, or nobody will dance with me, and I'll just spend the night standing against the wall." He sighed a very long breath and waited.

Knowing how many females watched Klyn's swooning drama, Elizabeth shrugged and said, "Well, I guess I'll have to be there."

Klyn added, "And you'll save me a dance."

Elizabeth considered him. Then she sighed gently and replied, "Okay," As if she'd endure him for one dance.

He took off his hat and fanned his face as though he was in panic. As though he was grateful she'd agreed to be at the dance that night.

She blushed and said just to him, "You're shocking."

He laughed.

So were the other young men smiling or laughing. Never before had the women actually stopped on the street and talked to the group of males. In that small town, too many adults watched. So the young women had been careful. But this time, Elizabeth had stopped by Klyn who was in the gathering of young males, so the other young women had been surprised, but they'd hesitated.

The males were so careful in their speech that it was amusing. The young men laughed and blushed. They could seem so rash, but with actual women there, they didn't know exactly how to act or what to do in those circumstances.

The males realized that Klyn was easy with the careful Elizabeth. He was easy with women. How'd he do that? And the startled, uncertain males slid their eyes over to Klyn. They were close enough to listen with one ear while they listened to the stopped females with the other.

Klyn said to Elizabeth, "You look terrific."

The other males heard that and they said the same damned words to the females in front of them. Fortunately, the young females weren't listening to the exchange between Klyn and Elizabeth. So the young women thought the boggled men were very clever and smooth.

Of course, the females knew they looked good. They'd put on how many outfits before they'd seen Elizabeth and put on a shirt and trousers as she had. With shoes, naturally. No socks. Just shoes...and their Stetsons.

Did they have on underwear? That was a wobbling undercurrent wonder of all the males along that part of the cross streets in the downtown part of that small town. It caused others to breathe a slow and tolerant sigh.

Since the stranger, Keeper, had asked Elizabeth to the dance, the males there awkwardly did the same thing with the other females. They asked, "Can you come to the dance?"

One of the females lifted her eyebrows and tilted her head as she retorted, "Are you asking for a date?"

Appalled by his lack of smoothness, the man said, "Yeah. Will ya?"

Kindly, she replied, "It would be a pleasure."

Another of the men told the young woman next to him, "Would you come with me?"

She asked, "Where?"

He clarified awkwardly, "To the dance."

She smiled and said, "I'd love it."

He was so wobbled that he said, "Me, too."

The others laughed, but they asked for dates, and only one female declined. The male was devastated. But the young woman told him, "I have to baby-sit the Tempkins' kids. Would you like to come over there? The kids are chaperones."

He laughed and said, "Let's bring the kids to the dance."

She tilted her head as she said, "I'll ask how late they can be awake."

He said, "I'll call you later?"

"My phone number is—"

"Wait. I'll write it down so's I don't louse up."

She laughed, but she blushed and was very pleased.

The females left with smiles. They were pink with blushes and they were animated.

The young men gathered together and said, "How'd this happen? They stopped and talked to us!"

Klyn blinked and replied, "What's so odd about that?"

"We've never been able to snare them in before this."

Klyn considered the whole situation as the guys talked on in amazement. Klyn said, "It was Elizabeth stopping to talk to me?"

"Yeah."

"Um-hmmm."

That did it.

And one said to Klyn, "We need you around so's we can snare in some more women."

They all agreed to that.

Klyn said seriously, "Behave."

That was all he said. And it covered all conduct. They listened. It wasn't going to be a donnybrook, but it ought to be interesting.

Finally, one of the guys asked, "What'd Elizabeth want?"

Klyn replied logically, "To go to the dance."

"She asked *you?*"

With some drama, Klyn emoted, "I'm a stranger in a strange land." How was *that* for evasion?

The men laughed.

Then Klyn asked, "Have you ever been away from home?"

None had. But why would they ever leave such a perfect place?

Klyn declared as he nodded his head, "You're gonna have to cross the canyon and visit the Keepers."

"Wow!"

They laughed and talked and planned.

It is odd how one person can change an area without knowing that he was the one responsible for the change.

Klyn phoned Elizabeth, and she was home. He asked, "What sort of flowers would you like for the dance?"

She asked in a puzzled way, "How do you mean?"

"Uh—in your hair? On your wrist? Where would you like to wear it?"

Elizabeth told him, "We really don't bother with flowers around here."

Klyn sighed gently and said, "I'll figure it out. What'll you wear?"

"Jeans?"

"May I escort you on my horses?"

"I'll be going with a bunch of girls. That way, we can do as we please."

"Save me a couple of dances?"

She replied, "I'll be there. You can stand in line."

He laughed softly and said, "Okay." He told her to behave and he hung up. Then he called some of the guys and asked, "Do we give the women flowers for the dance?"

The first one replied, "I hadn't really thought of that."

Klyn said, "Let's."

"Okay. I'll call a couple of the guys so's our dates won't be too isolated."

Klyn asked, "Isolated?" He'd heard no such

word used there and wasn't sure they recognized it.

The recipient of the call replied, "All the other females would be jealous."

Klyn suggested, "Maybe just a rose?"

"Yeah. Or a couple of flowers to pin to her shirt."

"Casual, huh?"

"Yeah. It's just a mixer. Nothing elaborate."

Klyn said offhandedly, "I'll see what I can find in the yards."

The man told Klyn, "Don't get caught."

Klyn laughed.

Klyn dressed casually, but he was still smoother than anyone else. He wore slacks and a long-sleeve turtleneck pullover. Everyone else wore denim for the evening dance. The interesting part was that Klyn wasn't uncomfortable. Even if he'd been a citizen there, he would have dressed his own way.

He'd brought a rose. A red one. And he gave it to Elizabeth. She smiled and put it in her hair.

The man with her didn't even look at Klyn, but watched Elizabeth. She didn't make a big deal out of the flower. But she did fix it in her hair so that it would survive.

Elizabeth had a line of willing males who waited for their turn to dance with her. They stood on the edge of the dance floor and watched and commented.

Klyn told the last man, "I get the dance after you, okay? I'll be off for a while, so don't forget me."

The guy laughed.

Klyn turned close to Elizabeth and said softly, "Behave."

Men tend to do that and it irritates the hell out of women. But think, there are women who are delighted a man is that possessive and aware of other men and how they act. So Elizabeth's face didn't change, but her eyes sparkled with delight.

Before Klyn's turn to dance with Elizabeth arrived, it was suppertime. Klyn had assumed he would escort her to the table, and he was shocked when some outcast said in a steely manner, "Buzz off"—to Klyn!

Klyn told the outcast, "She and I agreed we'd dine together."

The outcast retorted, "She and *me* dine together."

At that point, Elizabeth came along and heard

the outcast's speech. She asked, "Who's horning in?"

Both the outcast and Klyn said just about in unison, "He thinks he has you for dinner."

She was elaborately astonished and gasped, "Someone plans to eat me?"

The outcast said, "Him." Then he promised, "He won't get one bite of you. I'll see to that."

And the outcast could. That was what made Klyn hesitate in grabbing Elizabeth's arm and dragging her along with him. He didn't want to start a donnybrook. Who knew who all would side with...the outcast? Would a backup for that one be astonishing?

Then Klyn thought, How come Elizabeth was with the outcast? How in hell had she gotten involved with him?

So Klyn went off and found quite a few guys who were eating supper in a male group. There weren't that many females around loose.

However, one came to Klyn and asked, "All alone?"

He grinned and pretended he was chewing and not able to reply at that point. So the other guys there said, "How about one of us?"

So she stayed with them...and there were several other females who'd been found loose. They had a hilarious time. The women told how they'd been abandoned. They made a long funny joke out of the entire story.

Klyn wondered how they'd managed to sneak away from whoever and manage this kind of attention?

The men were laughing with the women, and as he laughed, Klyn glanced over and saw that Elizabeth was watching the group with a very grim look.

Klyn concentrated a little more on the entertaining women and didn't look again at Elizabeth.

But she came over to him and said very kindly, "This next dance is yours."

He said, "Glory be!" and stood up immediately.

Elizabeth stopped his rising and said, "The band isn't yet back."

Klyn grinned and said, "You can have half of my chair."

She said, "How generous."

He looked at her seriously and lifted his eyebrows as he asked, "Would you prefer half of my lap?"

"No."

That reply shocked him. He opened his mouth

to protest. Before he could do that, she sat on his immediately overexcited lap.

She listened to the exchanges among the others, and she laughed. She shifted her bottom. She kept his hands from moving wrong. Klyn was riveted. With her so close, he was very surprised that he could move or speak or do anything. But he did hold Elizabeth steady, and he did grasp her to prevent her from sliding down between his knees.

That just showed how important men are in monitoring loose females.

She got grapes and shared them with Klyn. Since his hands were so busy in holding her steady, Elizabeth had to feed him the grapes all by herself.

She managed the sharing of the grapes.

He kept her from falling between his knees.

As he adjusted again, she asked him softly, "Am I heavy?"

He replied softly, just to her, "You're slithery as a snake."

"I'm a *snake?*"

"You were probably in the Garden."

Indignantly, she protested, "I was not! I was dancing the entire time!"

He was patient and explained, "Back in the days of Adam and Eve."

"*That* garden?"

"Yeah."

"Oh." She considered. "Was I Eve?"

"You were probably some other female who was watching and getting involved."

"Poor Adam."

Klyn sighed and looked aside in a rather irritated manner.

"What's wrong with Adam?"

Klyn frowned. "Women tend to feel sorry for Adam. Think of Eve!"

Logically, Elizabeth mentioned, "She was a woman."

He agreed, "Yeah."

"So." She waited.

"They were the only two people in the world."

She shook her head. "That's not so. They were new people. How did they find others?"

"Different people?"

She replied, "Yeah. Adam and Eve were just beginners of a new strain."

"What would you think if I told you the men here think you're…different." He watched her.

"I am."

He told her softly, "I care about you."

She told him, "You took your horse and left me."

Very gently, he told her, "I was already late for a meeting I'd arranged. You waylaid me."

"Way...laid?" She looked off and considered the words.

"You lured me so that I forgot all those men who were gathering to hear what I had to say."

She smiled and said, "It's because I care about you, too."

Seven

Having danced with most of the women, the men began to mention that they'd be glad to escort the ladies home. Klyn had right away asked Elizabeth for that privilege. She'd hesitated before she said, "I'd be delighted."

As they walked to the car, Elizabeth looked for the horses. They were nowhere to be found. She asked, "It's a distance to walk?"

He told her, "This is the car I've rented for tonight."

Elizabeth gasped in amazement and surprise. She said, "How astute of you."

He was modest.

The two got into the front seat of the car Klyn had rented with the money he'd carefully saved. The car worked very well, but then Klyn was skilled and gentle.

That was probably what caught Elizabeth's attention. She sat next to Klyn because, she said, she wanted to watch how to drive.

That quick nugget of wit made Klyn laugh. He'd learned that Elizabeth had been driving since she was eight. Even back then, at that age, Elizabeth had been smart. Her parents had turned her loose on their land. She hadn't hit even one tree, but she'd run out of gas. Even that was while she was on the way back from where she'd been practicing. And once she'd mired the wheels in sand. She'd tried a shortcut. Her daddy had used the mules to drag out the stuck car.

In comparison, Klyn's driving was boring.

Klyn said in an aloof manner, "I'm legit."

After she'd started to laugh, Elizabeth gasped and said, "I'm not?"

Klyn said, "I'll have to see." But he slid his eyes over and just looked wickedly at Elizabeth. "I'm in favor of you being along. With me."

Elizabeth said, "You're a remarkable escort."

He replied instantly, "Thank you."

She laughed, while the prairie wolf just licked his smiling lips as if he was tasting something remarkable.

Klyn asked, "Want to ride a while?"

Elizabeth told Klyn, "I can't be alone with a prairie wolf."

Klyn turned his head to look at her with great interest and asked, "Who's a prairie wolf?"

Coyly, Elizabeth retorted, "I've known him for several days."

Klyn responded, "Ohhh, that's not long. A bit more contact, and you'll know him better." Klyn coughed once to stop the laugh. He was very careful.

Men are clever and sly.

Elizabeth wasn't quite sure what all was happening. It seemed to her that her protective walls were loose and unsteady. They could fall down. Then what was she to do? She lifted her eyebrows and licked her lips so that she didn't smile.

As Klyn drove down the road, she pointed out places she'd used for various things.

Klyn inquired, "What...various things?"

"Dollhouses, Tarzan trees, smooching places."

And *he* said, "Ah-hah!"

Elizabeth laughed.

Klyn asked, "Where are your kin?"

"My older sisters are at their new homes, taking care of the children while their husbands are out, finding out what's going on in the area."

He heard her bitterness. Klyn said, "Men work all day, mostly alone, and they have to find out what's going on in the area. They need to know." His voice was soft and earnest.

That boggled Elizabeth. She didn't accept Klyn's premise, but she was wobbled. They were silent. It was Klyn who mentioned, "Where's the next dance to be?"

"At the same place. We do that so we can all see each other."

He asked, "I can go?"

"Only if you have a date. If we don't stress that, men come alone and look to see what available women are there. We charge them double."

He nodded. "I can see that."

Elizabeth reminded him, "You have to take a date."

"Oh."

With some surprise, Elizabeth asked, "Something wrong with men dating?"

"No."

There was silence in the car. Elizabeth looked slowly to her left and gave Klyn a look.

He looked over at her. She was adjusting the seat harness. Klyn considered her. She seemed different.

He guided the car and drove Elizabeth to her house. He said, "You're home."

She looked at him again. Then she got out of the car.

Klyn got out the other side and waited to walk with her.

However, she went off ahead of him, across the sidewalk, up the porch steps and opened the front door. She didn't say one word as she lifted her chin. She went inside and closed the door softly.

He turned and walked back to the car. He got in and started the engine then eased away, his thoughts centered on Elizabeth.

Tired and sleepy, Klyn returned the car to the rental dealer. Then he walked to his hotel and went to his room.

So Klyn called Elizabeth the next afternoon and asked lazily, "How are you?"

She replied, "I was up until after two. I wrote letters."

"Who'd you write to?"

She said, "My grandmother, my cousin, a school chum. Why do you ask?"

Klyn said, "No...lover?"

Elizabeth said, "I do have a potential...for writing."

So Klyn asked, "How does a man get...suitable? What sort of suits does he wear?"

Elizabeth's laughter slid into her reply. "You could buy a guitar and sit outside on the porch and thumb and sing?"

He replied, "I'll see if that wo—"

Elizabeth interrupted, "There are other ways."

He was curious. "What would those be?"

"You could come over for lunch. My little nephews will be here and you can discipline their manners."

Klyn said thoughtfully, "I can do that."

"Come about eleven-thirty?"

Klyn asked, "It somehow escaped me, but are you a good cook?"

She replied loftily, "I can do peanut butter sandwiches that you wouldn't believe."

Klyn asked Elizabeth, "How come you'll accept me now, when I was so rejected last night?''

''I've known you in many ways for some long time.''

Klyn said, ''Ahhhh. I see.''

Elizabeth replied, ''Maybe you don't...yet. I'll look for you about...eleven-thirty?''

''I'll be there.''

He put the phone gently onto its stand and sat thoughtfully. He needed someone else there. His acquaintance with Elizabeth could pick up and he'd find himself caught by her. So he'd call his brother, Tala. Tala was older and wiser and he knew women. He was one hell of a man.

Klyn thought for several minutes and wondered if Tala would snatch up that young female jewel, and poor old Klyn would never see her again...alone.

Maybe it would be better if Klyn found out just how stable Elizabeth was. Maybe he ought to know if she was still taken by him, or if another man could sway her.

He'd better have another look at her before he or somebody else did anything rash.

So Klyn put on jeans with a blue work shirt. He didn't wear a tie, but he wore a red bandanna around his throat. He used the buffer on his boots.

His hair could use a clipping. He felt his chin to be sure he'd gotten all the whiskers. He breathed as he watched himself in the mirror. The face watching him was sober and fairly calm.

He could handle anything.

He went riding on one of his horses. And the other horse just went along. They needed the exercise, and he'd just see what Elizabeth thought about riding the other one.

He'd given himself time, so he got to the Moores' at eleven-thirty. Right on the dot. He hadn't even had to stay under a tree somewhere to kill time. But he had allowed the horse to slack and try the weeds.

Elizabeth came to the door with some little nephews who were curious. They nodded during the introductions. Klyn saw that Elizabeth was blushing a tad. He liked that. She wasn't the calm, cool person she sometimes appeared.

She said to her nephews under her breath, "We'll not be eating for almost half an hour. You all go along, and I'll call you when it's time to eat."

The youngest, who was four, looked up at her,

as would a very short adult, and said, "I'll stay."

The others said something similar. All were watching Klyn.

With courtesy, Klyn said, "I haven't known you all. Tell me about your family."

The eldest child replied, "Our great grand-daddy came here from the other side of TEXAS." And he added soberly, "TEXAS is always—"

"—in caps. I know that one." Klyn grinned.

The nephew asked, "You heard that?"

Klyn said, "Yep."

"We generally tell people that, and they're surprised."

Klyn told the boys, "They haven't been here with the family long enough."

"How long you been here?" one of her nephews asked.

"Over five hundred years."

In delighted surprise, one of the boys said, "Wow! You're five hundred?"

One of the other nephews said, "The new ones are probably all Yankees."

Klyn nodded thoughtfully and agreed. "That could be so. We call them Winter TEXANS."

One of the boys said, "It's a change to have

a TEXAN here. Aunt Elizabeth doesn't always find TEXANS. She just brings home old cats or dogs that've been left at the end of the Northern winter."

Klyn's eyes twinkled as he looked at Elizabeth. He asked, "Oh?"

So naturally, with that encouragement, all three boys gave out family secrets. One said, "She helps at the old folks' home. She brings home people and animals, and the family endures."

Now how many people, let alone children, use the word endure? Klyn nodded once slowly to share that…endurance.

Elizabeth was tolerant. She allowed the boys to take over and chatter. They loved company. Klyn was company.

Then they saw his horses!

They went out to be sure the horses were comfortable and had enough to eat, then the boys petted the horses. Of course, the boys wanted to ride them, but Elizabeth said, "No."

Klyn raised his eyebrows gently and looked at Elizabeth. She was sternly watching her nephews. They smiled at her.

How clever of them.

After the meal at which all the boys talked at

once and were kept in line by their very stern aunt, dessert did come. The boys never said a thing as they gobbled up the ice cream and cookies. They smiled at Elizabeth, and then at Klyn, and when they were finished, they left.

Silence dropped.

Elizabeth asked Klyn, "Can you still hear out of your overused ears?"

Klyn had the nerve to say, "What's that?" as he curled a hand around his ear.

Elizabeth sighed and lay back in her chair.

Klyn asked, "You take a nap after lunch?"

"Yes! I'm exhausted. Thank you so much for all the replies and explanations you gave the boys. They think you're quite adult and that your brain works. Most people's brains are dead."

"Are they now." He licked his smile.

"I believe parents pretend their brains are dead so that they don't have to listen to their offsprings' arguing."

"The boys didn't argue when they were eating," Klyn mentioned.

"That's because they spent the time seeing if you knew anything at all. They asked questions to which they knew the reply."

"How shocking."

Elizabeth laughed. "I know. It was even in-

teresting for me to listen to you. You were very
patient. And you knew the replies that were cor-
rect, and you questioned the ones you knew
were wrong.''

''I have brothers older than I.''

Elizabeth laughed again.

Klyn told her, ''You probably have the best
laugh I've ever heard from a woman.''

She lifted her eyebrows and said softly, ''You
did very well.''

He told her, ''I know about lunch guests who
are raked over the coals by young ones. You
need to know that I have not only brothers, but
sisters!''

She lifted her eyebrows again and said,
''Wow.''

He was disgruntled. ''That wasn't very
shocked.''

''I was curious how you'd handled my nephews since you did exceptionally well.'' Elizabeth
told him seriously, ''You handled it all su-
perbly.''

He said kindly, ''I'd like to just handle you.''

She blushed as she gasped and then laughed.

So, of course, he asked, ''Would you like to
see how I'd handle you?''

She went sober-faced and silent, then ventured carefully, "You're more than you appear."

He shook his head slowly. "No. I'm honest and ordinary."

She burst out laughing. "You're...*normal?* Is *that* what you think?"

He considered her words thoughtfully. "I'm just a man."

She put her head back and laughed, then she gasped, *"You?"* And she laughed some more.

He smiled tolerantly as he asked, "Why do you think it's funny?"

She settled down, still smiling, then she looked at him, and he was waiting for a reply. She sobered. She asked, "Don't you know?"

"Not a clue."

"You're a very different man. You'll enjoy this. It's the truth. You probably hear it so often that you can pretend it's all news to you. But you are a remarkable man. No. Don't guide me. Let me tell you what I know.

"I've spent time with you. I saw you when you were talking to the other men. You had their attention. You're a speaker. I wonder if the women would respond to you alertly and not just smile and wiggle."

He shook his head.

She continued, "I do hope you solve your mission, and I do hope the culprit is found before any of you is hurt. Especially you. I find you a very special man."

He had listened. He had watched her. Now he said to her, "How about loving me?"

She looked at him.

He smiled a tad. "I'll give you more room to decide. I'll give you time."

"Yes."

"You've been completely honest with me. You've told me exactly what you think. Now I'm asking you to consider me."

She watched him cautiously. "This is rash."

"So was bringing a man to a table with young nephews who were curious and questioning."

She tilted her head. "You disliked it all?"

"The table was well done, the boys were alert and curious. You're an intelligent woman. You're the one I want. Are you willing? You have been open with me. I am returning the logic. I want you."

She replied, "You've been with other women."

Klyn asked, "Is that a shock when a man is my age?"

She blushed but stayed serious. She told him, "I've not been...intimate with a man."

He told her softly, "I can't believe I've found you."

She asked seriously, "Have you? Or do you just think I'm now...different."

He told her gently, "You're what men think they'll find, but seldom do."

She chided, "If you speak like that, you will spoil me rotten."

He smiled. "Okay."

"Now why do you think spoiling me rotten is okay?"

"I would see."

So she asked with curiosity, "What is it that you'd see?"

"You."

Elizabeth told him, "I believe that this is all too sudden. We should back off and regard each other more seriously."

So Klyn asked softly, "Would you regard me?"

"You waggle my understanding and control."

He inquired kindly but quite seriously, "Is that bad?"

"Just this afternoon, I was in full control. What have you done to me?"

He echoed what she asked, "What have I done to you?"

She shook her head. "I no longer feel in control of myself."

"Who controls you?"

She looked at him and her eyes were quite serious. "I'm no longer sure of it being me."

"I need to kiss you."

"No."

He smiled softly. "Why not?"

"I don't think this is a good time for you to do something like that to me. I'm not stable." Soberly, she elaborated, "I'm not sure I can handle that right now."

He coaxed, "Just a kiss?"

Her breathing was strange. She felt a little insecure. The house was too silent. Where were her nephews? She watched Klyn and breathed carefully. She licked her lips. Then she blotted them with a handkerchief from her pocket.

He asked, "Now?"

Quite earnestly, she said, "I don't believe I can handle this right now, right here. I think we ought to go outside and look at your horses." She sat straight and pushed her chair back with her feet. She rose...

...and he reached to move back her chair.

It helped for him to do that for her.

They went out of the room and crossed the hall to the living room. There, they went to the row of glass doors and out onto the porch.

No one was anywhere around. No human sound reached them. They went across the porch and down the steps onto a cement walk.

The trees were beautiful and lazy in the sun. They were precious trees long ago planted by her great-grandparents. She told Klyn that.

He commented that his own family of Keepers had been in their area for a long old time.

"I've heard that. How many of you all have moved away?"

He replied easily enough, "Some. But the best stay around." He smiled at her. She was a remarkable woman. His stomach clenched. What if she refused him now?

Klyn took her hand in his and walked along silently because he was unsure what all she wanted to hear. He waited.

She asked, "Do you love me?"

"Yes. You're special."

She asked, "How can you know that?"

"I watch and listen. I know you."

Elizabeth asked carefully, "Do you think I

love you?'' And she watched him with enormous eyes and a very serious mouth.

He replied, ''Not yet.''

''Not...yet?''

''—but you could.''

Elizabeth frowned at the ground before she asked, ''How can you know that?''

''I asked God.''

She looked away and took a deep breath.

Klyn asked softly, ''Would you like to hear what God said to me about you?''

She lifted her nose and said, ''Baloney.''

Klyn shook his head slowly as he replied, ''I'm serious. Wanna hear?''

She walked a tad, then her curiosity got the better of her and she turned back to him and asked, ''Okay. What?''

''God said, 'She could be the one.'''

Elizabeth sighed with patience and asked, ''Just like that?''

Klyn nodded soberly and repeated, ''Just like that.''

''Baloney.''

They had arrived in the area where Klyn had left his two horses. The boys were there and the horses were being fed Johnson grass. Their nibbles were dainty.

Klyn said to the boys, "You are very kind to the horses. Would you like to ride them? Not too rough and not too far."

The boys became excited and looked to their aunt for approval. Elizabeth relented, knowing how skilled her older nephews were with horses and knowing how excited they were to ride Klyn's. The littlest one was old enough to ride alone, but he went with his big brother, and the middle brother had one horse to himself. They rode off.

Left alone again, Klyn looked over at Elizabeth. She ran her tongue over her lower lip, then stood straight and looked right at him.

He smiled at her.

She was very serious.

He said softly, "Hello, love."

Eight

It is not only boggling to find there is love, it is exuberant, or it could be one-sided and a disaster.

Klyn Keeper asked his love, Elizabeth, "Are you real?"

She tilted her head thoughtfully and replied, "I think so."

They walked along her parents' land and Klyn said, "I love to look at you and hold your hand."

She laughed softly.

"I really ought to be on my knees, but I suppose that would hamper you a tad?"

She replied, "Probably." Then she asked with interest, "Was it attraction or was it despair that's made you love me. Have you looked around?"

He replied with some subtle humor, "I have looked around. My daddy told me that I ought to see some of the world before I got married and had a passel of kids...and then saw my dream."

She nodded.

But then he told her that she was a beautiful woman, that he wouldn't hesitate loading her with children. He'd *like* doing it, but he worried about her having to have the baby and do most of the caretaking.

She lifted her hand, then put the back of it to her forehead and said in some haunting manner, "It takes a whole lot from a woman."

He loved it.

As they walked along, Klyn spoke again about the bullets that came over onto Keeper land across the canyon.

Klyn said, "We seriously believe the shooter is not trying for us. He shoots at the cliff, but sometimes the bullet goes over the top and rides along pretty low—''

''I don't know of any—''

Klyn told her kindly, ''I'm not pushing at you, honey. I'm thinking aloud to solve this mystery and tidy it up. The last bullet caused a good man to be injured.''

Elizabeth nodded. ''I've heard about that.'' She shrugged as her face continued to express concern. ''A lot of us shoot across the canyon.''

He nodded in agreement. ''I'm telling you why I'm here. But actually, I'm boggled by you.''

She sassed, ''I boggle you?''

''Only now and then. Remember when I told you to become a congresswoman and go to Washington? You're a speaker, too. People respond to you.''

''It would be a challenge. But I doubt I could leave here.''

He nodded. ''The kids.''

She laughed.

''Actually, I believe you would be honest and completely involved.''

Elizabeth looked at Klyn.

He said easily, ''You'd throw yourself into

the middle of whatever and get things done for this area. You're a doer.''

''I'm glad you told me that. I've wondered if you were just a woman-hopper.''

He licked his smile and looked off as men tend to do. He said, ''I believe you are all any man would need, and you are mine. Do you want me? I'd be loyal and I'd survive.'' He continued to look around and said, ''All that I tell you is true. This isn't any sideline or guess. I know what I'm talking about.''

Elizabeth said, ''How gentle you are.''

He was rather elaborately astonished. ''You like men...rough?''

She shook her head as she laughed.

On impulse Klyn hustled Elizabeth over into some bushes.

She said to him seriously, ''There'll be three young males searching for me in three minutes.''

He looked so innocent! He said, ''I wanted you to see this bird nest.'' And he showed her the new little bird that wobbled its neck and opened his big, hungry mouth.

Elizabeth was enchanted. She said, ''Don't touch anything. The mother may abandon it.''

So he eased her out of the mass and walked

along with her as if everyone looked for bird nests.

He looked around the area as he had been doing all along, and he said, "Don't you have a river of some kind around these parts? How'm I gonna lay myself down on this red bug-invaded grass with my head in your lap and snooze a trifle in the shade? Your perfect lunch has made me sleepy, it was all so good and filling."

"You wiggled out of that one just right. You are careful."

He mentioned, "The river?"

And she said, "Sitting down and allowing you to snore for a time with your heavy head holding my lap in place is a dead bore. I'll lie down and put *my* head in *your* lap."

He said slyly, "You could be very surprised."

Elizabeth told him, "I know exactly what you imply. Remember that I am very aware of male problems. They are so obvious."

So Klyn asked, "How come us males are like that? So obvious."

She laughed, blushing, shaking her head.

He grinned, watching her. He said, "How about marrying me legally tomorrow and us getting intimately acquainted?"

She looked at him and gasped. Then she lifted

her nose a tad and said with dignity, "You are supposed to be more aware of your comments, sir. You are absolutely—"

He kissed her, then he lifted his mouth from hers and smiled. She was boggled and unable to adjust herself. He said, "You're something."

She took a while to ask, "What's that mean?"

"You got in the car last night, and I didn't want you to get out."

Elizabeth's eyes were closed and she was limp against him. She said, "I thought I'd escaped you." She indicated that, in leaving, she was safe.

He told her, "It never works. If the man is sharp enough, he'll do anything to keep her."

Elizabeth frowned and her mouth worked, then she managed, "Keep...her? That's your name!"

Klyn sighed. "It makes one wonder how the family got such a name, doesn't it?"

Still not able to straighten herself, Elizabeth managed to mention, "It's no surprise."

So he inquired gently, "What is the surprise? I hadn't known of any."

"The Keepers keep women."

Klyn nodded. He looked off and nodded

again. He said, "Yeah, that about covers it all. I guess it is no surprise."

"How long have Keeper men been doing that?"

"Keeping women?"

She mentioned slowly, "Ye-ah."

"Probably about as long as other men do the same thing. We aren't alone in liking women around."

She asked, "To do all the work?"

He replied, "To sit on a cushion and sew a fine seam?"

"I've heard of that." She opened her eyes. She said, "There's the sky."

He glanced up. "Have you been searching for it?"

Elizabeth considered. "It's up there. I'd been looking for the snake in the grasses."

So Klyn asked with interest, "Are you a civilized woman."

"Since school."

He was curious. "Where did you go?"

"We have no women's school's here. Daddy was opposed to us girls going to the mixed schools. He doesn't trust other males. So Mother sent us off to women's schools."

Klyn nodded. "I can see that."

Elizabeth looked at Klyn with some interest. "You don't trust males?"

He nodded and immediately added to her sentence, "—with women."

"Why ever not?"

So he told her, "As a man grows and matures, he realizes women should be schooled without men."

"Baloney. That's why we're put in female schools?" She pulled herself into a manner of collection and put her hands to her head.

Klyn asked, "What's baloney about men and women studying separately?"

"Have you ever seen a man who has studied in an all-male place? Or a female who has done the same thing? They turn out sex hungry!"

He took a step backward and gasped, "No!"

"Yes! And the very minute— You are mocking me."

He grinned. "I'd *never* do a thing like that."

"You are teasing me."

Klyn asked her, "Have you ever known of any real man who isn't aware of a beautiful female?"

"Most men always look at women. But if you will notice, there are women who look at men."

Klyn whispered, "That is shocking!"

She stopped and observed him. She said, "You've teased and taunted and listened to me. You're not at all concerned about men wanting women."

"I'm a man."

Elizabeth was impatient. "I've noticed."

"Those who are really men notice women. They are such remarkable creatures that we all love them. They are magic."

Elizabeth asked, "What about the women who are married and don't care about having a strange man watching them."

Klyn promised, "She doesn't mind if he isn't intrusive. If he's just watching and not blowing steam, he's okay."

"I don't believe that." She said it thoughtfully. "A woman doesn't like to be viewed unless she is interested in the man. Otherwise, she just wants a husband."

"Some do."

"There are women who don't particularly care for their husbands, or husbands who don't pay any attention to their wives. Those aren't good marriages."

Klyn told her, "I'd like to be with you. Why are you wobbling?"

"Because." But then she said, "How do I

know that it would be forever? You could easily get bored with me or distracted by another woman. You're out here, away from your family, and you're alone."

"I'll look around at what else is available." He tilted his head and inquired, "Will you wait until I decide?"

She watched him. "I think you'd be worth the wait."

Klyn tilted his head back as he closed his eyes. He gasped, "You ought not to be so open. You're driving me out of my mind."

Elizabeth told him, "We were talking seriously. You're very vulnerable or you're...ready. And any willing woman would do...for now."

"It's *you*. *You* drive me crazy. Why not be kind to me now?"

"I haven't done one single thing to attract you. You have been with other women, no question. I believe it's just that I'm an available female in a place that's rather isolated."

Klyn told her, "There're a lot of women around. I have looked. I found you."

So Elizabeth asked him, "Who will you see next?"

He watched her soberly, then he told her, "We'll see."

"What are you saying? That you'll cotton to me unless some other woman turns up who lures you?"

"I don't believe that would be at all right. I have never felt what I feel for you. I could love you for the rest of my life."

"How long has it been since you've been here?" she asked him. "Has your mind decided that's long enough?"

He smiled.

She said, "You're very alluring to any woman. And you are skilled. I know. I could be drawn into your net."

"Okay."

After a minute, Elizabeth said softly, "I believe that I want to be with you...intimately. Then you would either love me, or you would become restless and look elsewhere."

He told her seriously, with no humor at all, "I could love you without using your body. I know what I want, what I've looked for. It is you."

She said, "We'll see."

Klyn said softly, "Kiss me. Let me hold you against me. I long for you."

She hesitated. But she wanted the same things

even if he wasn't permanent. They would create memories for cold nights and bleak days.

She lifted her arms to hold him, and his arms slid around her, drawing her body close to his. He groaned in a delicious wanting and held her softness against him. Then he kissed her as she should be kissed.

Klyn put his head close, next to hers, and just held her to his body. He said, "You're so soft."

That startled her. Men were so different, tough and hard, with no softness to them. She was...soft? She hadn't known that.

But she did know she'd always liked Klyn's body. She said to him, "Let's do it."

Hugging her, relishing her softness, Klyn asked with closed eyes, "What do you want to do?"

"Let's...well, let's...make...love."

He went entirely still. Then he asked very gently, "Do you really want to?"

Her eyes popped open and she exclaimed, "I don't have any condoms!"

He told her, "Neither do I. I don't think. I might have one in my wallet." Reluctantly, he began to release her.

He pulled out his wallet. "Let me check it out...." He gasped. "By golly, I do have one!"

Elizabeth gasped rather oddly and said, "How fortunate!"

Klyn asked gently, "Are you sure?"

She managed to say, "I think so."

Klyn said, "You know I wouldn't hurt you for anything in this world." And he meant it. He hesitated with the enormity of the moment.

Elizabeth noted that his breathing was strange. He was uncertain? She said, "It'll be okay." She wondered what had happened to make him hesitate.

He looked at her with startled, naked eyes.

She smiled and put her hand on the upper part of his arm. She said softly, "Don't worry."

He kissed her sweetly, gently, and then their kisses turned urgent, passionate. When he unzipped his trousers, he said to her, "I'm not sure about this—uh—condom. It's been a long time, so I'm not sure exactly how it works. Could you help me?"

She looked at him then and said, "Let me see—" She gasped. She told him, "It's so big. I'd never known how big it is."

Klyn replied earnestly, "Do you think so?"

"It's so big," she said again.

He looked down and said, "Let's just put it

between your thighs and see how that feels...for us.''

She blushed and they went into the bushes for privacy. They found that other people—or creatures—had been there at odd times. The grass was quite worn.

Elizabeth said, ''We can't try it here. Someone might come.''

He coughed. Several times.

She said, ''Let's find another place.''

He coughed again.

She hesitated and asked, ''Are you catching a summer cold?''

He shook his head as he gently eased his shirttails out of his jeans to cover himself. It was hardly sly, walking with his shirt out thataway.

Pointing to much denser brush, Elizabeth asked, ''How about here?'' She was moving her head, looking around very seriously. She said, ''Hurry! Get inside!''

Klyn gasped and straightened as he put a hand over his heart.

She explained kindly but hurriedly, ''Some of the boys might come by.''

He said a very shocked, ''Oh!'' And he said, ''Hurry!'' And he hustled her right under the enormous bush. He said kindly, "When we're married, I'll grow all our bushes high."

"Why?" She was curious.

He suggested, "So we can be together and never worry about anyone finding us."

Elizabeth smiled and pulled off her panties.

Klyn told her, "You probably ought to take off that dress so that it doesn't get too wrinkled."

Elizabeth stopped and thought about that, then she said, "Oh." And she shucked the dress, shaking it out and laying it carefully aside.

Klyn said, "And the bra."

"All right." She was breathing rather quickly, her eyes large.

He took off his trousers very carefully, and put them aside on top of his shirt and boots. Then he took off his underwear.

He smiled at her. She was lovely.

Klyn kissed her very gently. He held her to him and he breathed. He said, "Are you all right?"

She nodded in little bobs.

"Your body is so soft. Feel mine."

So she put her hand on his chest.

He said, "Lower."

She slid her hand down. She mentioned seriously, "It's daytime. We're outside!"

He smiled. She was precious. He gently pulled her closer to him, against him...and he kissed her.

Elizabeth said, "You really know how to kiss."

"Hadn't you noticed that?" He pulled his head back and smiled down at her. He held her against his chest and smoothed his hand down her back. He said, "You're enticing to a man. He sees you and he wants to love you."

She didn't move, but her tiny, thin voice wobbled as she said, "I haven't ever done this!"

He held her body very tightly against his taut, smooth one and said, "You're beautiful," then he kissed her very seriously. His hand moved and he petted her. His throat made sounds of pleasure. He told her, "You're really something."

She was pleased. Her breathing was different. She moved so that he could touch her chest. He rolled her breasts with a large hand and squeezed one gently as he shivered with want.

She asked, "Now?"

He agreed, "I want to make love to you."

"I want to make love to you, too."

He lifted her across his chest and held her against him. He talked softly to her, telling her how beautiful she was and how wonderful it was for his hand to move on her, for his mouth to be able to kiss her, for his body to feel her against him.

When he entered her, carefully, gently, he said, "You're beautiful."

She was startled. "My face?"

"All of you. You're so graceful and female. You're really something."

She gazed into his eyes and smiled.

Nine

"**M**ove over here, close to me," Klyn said, his voice quiet and very intimate. His body was anxious.

Elizabeth moved over a bit and watched him. "We really should start looking for the boys. They've been riding for a little while now."

Klyn took Elizabeth into his arms and held her against him. He kissed her so that her face was stable but her brain twirled around inside her skull. It did.

"Don't worry. We will."

Elizabeth had never experienced anything like

or even similar to lovemaking with Klyn. It was somewhat boggling. She had some difficulty in managing herself...how was she supposed to act?

She'd get that figured out...sometime.

Elizabeth found that Klyn did all sorts of things with his mouth to her mouth and to her body parts. She was surprised and delighted and shocked. She would say, "Is that legal?"

And Klyn would murmur, "Ummmm," for whatever that meant.

Elizabeth gasped and her eyes were either almost closed or they were wide and shocked. She would say, "Uhhh," and she said, "Mmmmm." And she held breaths almost too long.

He just went right on making sweet love to her.

She exclaimed, "How'd you know...to do such a thing?" She'd ask, "Who told you to do something like that?" She'd said, "Who on *earth* taught you to—" And she whispered, "Yes."

Klyn just made soft, calming sounds, and he soothed her with his busy hands.

That was...soothing? He was driving her clear around the mental bend!

Elizabeth gasped. She breathed. That was a

good thing—if she'd held her breath, she would have passed out. So she did breathe and gasp and opened her mouth as if to say something, but she rarely did. Whatever he was doing, it was different from anything she'd ever had done to her body.

It was shocking.

It was marvelous.

She wanted more.

More of...what?

In no time at all, he lay her on her back and slid over her until he was settled exactly right. Then, on top of her, he told her, "Slide my sex into you."

Her eyes went very large and blank. She gasped but said, "Okay."

Klyn shivered as he sank his excited sex into her. He breathed. He gasped.

She told him, "Wow."

He soothed, "Yeah."

She moved her hands. She was impressed.

He moved.

Elizabeth said, "More!"

Klyn said, "Curl your hips and bend your knees up."

She wasn't at all sure she could even do all that, but she did try, and it did work!

Klyn sank deeper into her and his sounds were ragged and hoarse. He said, ''Ahhh, mmmmm,'' and his breathing was especially concerning to her. He was panting.

She began to move along with Klyn. As he pulled away from her, she moved her body to allow him to leave, but when he came back against her in a powerful thrust, she was surprised that she moved forward to accept him.

Then Klyn did that same thing again. Out and back. It was amazing. Suddenly, he gasped, went rigid, and slid down until he was just weight on her.

Elizabeth's intimate muscles squeezed him as she found her own release. She looked at Klyn with anxious eyes and said, ''Are you all right?''

Without opening his eyes or replying, he smiled.

That was all he did. Slowly, his face relaxed...and he began to snore. She was appalled. Someone might hear him! Elizabeth moved his lax body onto its side so the snore wouldn't be so blatant.

The things a woman has to do!

*   *   *

It was almost a half hour later that Klyn wakened and looked over to the restless and wide-eyed Elizabeth.

She smiled. She asked, "Are we going to do it again?"

He crossed his eyes and pretended to slide back into oblivion.

She reached over to waggle his face and said, "Don't do that. It's my turn."

That startled Klyn. *Her* turn? He said, "I did the best I could. I'm...drained."

So she asked avidly, "How soon can you do it again?"

He touched her cheek gently before his hand dropped down next to her. He was exhausted. In the next moment, he put his hand over her mouth as he said, "Shhhh" very quietly.

A little voice was saying close by, "—must of gone back to the house."

Another young voice replied, "Yeah."

And then the voices and the grass-swishing steps moved off.

The lovers didn't waste any time getting back into their clothes. Dressed, Klyn rolled Elizabeth close in his arms and just held her. It was very frustrating to her. Her hungry body was just about wild.

Klyn said, "Soon..." For whatever that meant.

They moved out of their hiding place carefully. She waited as Klyn ordered the weeds...enough. They left the precious area and walked gently toward the house.

He held her hand. He lifted it to his mouth and kissed it. He watched her. She breathed through her mouth to be silent. He told her she was so beautiful that she scared him.

"Balderdash."

Klyn squinched up his face as he considered the word. Then he told her, "I didn't know anyone said that anymore."

Restlessly, Elizabeth explained, "My grandmother does. It's better than cursing."

On the walk to Elizabeth's house, Klyn stopped to show her things like bird nests, or slinking creatures. He told her, "We're always called the intruders...and we probably are."

She could see that.

Gradually, Elizabeth became calmer. She allowed him to hold her hand, and she didn't crush his fingers. Her cheeks were again pale. She breathed normally.

He found a rill and took off his boots to wade. He invited her to join him, and she did.

He told her, "Our clothes are just a tad wrinkled, and we need to seem careless...watching the creatures and wading."

Elizabeth replied, "How clever of you. How did you come to know all that?" And she looked at him in a level and suspicious manner.

Klyn automatically looked around the area for who or whatever might be there as he told her, "This information has been passed down by the Keeper daddies to all the male youngsters in the family."

"Not the females?"

"Males take care of females. This is the way to do it."

"Ahhhhh."

Klyn told her, "Most young ladies don't realize how they look after they've been with a man. She tends to hold his hand and lean against him. It's a dead giveaway."

"I see."

He mentioned, "It's accepted for newlyweds to do that sort of thing."

"But not us?" Elizabeth looked at him.

"We're not married."

She straightened and looked around. She told him, "This has been a charming walk. Thank you."

Then she sloshed out of the rill and went on up the bank. She slid her shoes on her wet feet. Then she started walking toward the house.

Klyn called, "Now wait a minute. How come— Don't leave me here alone! I'll get scared!" He grinned.

She looked over her shoulder at him in dismissal and said, "The house is that way." And she walked in that direction.

He laughed as he hurried out of the water and pulled on his boots without socks, which he put into his pocket. He ran after her to catch up. Klyn said, "I didn't put on my socks. I'll probably get raw rubs."

Elizabeth said, "Probably."

And he told her quietly, "Settle down."

Elizabeth glanced over at him in elaborate surprise and said, "I'm perfectly balanced. Don't be concerned. It's okay that you didn't want to be with me again."

Klyn took hold of her arm and stopped her. He said, "You're mistaken. I'm trying very hard so that you will appear as if you've only been wading. Now don't you get feisty with me," he chided gently.

She tilted her head. Her expression was of an adult female who is really ticked. She said, "Of course. The house is in that direction.'' And she left him.

He caught up with her again. "What's the real problem? That I couldn't make love to you again? You have no idea what you're like to a hungry man. I have no control over the want of you. I'll make it up to you.''

She smiled. "No need." Then she waved to someone and called, "Hold up. I'm coming!" She turned and said to him, "I'll probably see you at the house.'' Then she ran off to some of her sisters.

But as she got to them, the women were looking beyond her and smiled just a tad. She looked back, and Klyn was only about five steps behind her. He wasn't even breathing harshly...as she was.

It didn't take the women any time at all to realize the couple *was* a couple. They waved and said, "See you later.'' And they went on off with Elizabeth's nephews.

Just like that.

Elizabeth then walked toward the house alone. However, Klyn caught up with her again. He took her hand and said seriously, "We have to solve this. What exactly did I do wrong?''

"You rejected me.''

Klyn shook his head and his face was very serious. "Honey, I could never reject you. I was telling you how we'd act to fool the others until we know what we're doing. We have to be careful."

Elizabeth tilted her head as she moved her arm for release. "Don't worry about me. I do understand. I wish I had...sooner."

He took hold of her other wrist and held her, keeping her from leaving him again. Watching her eyes with interest, he said, "Elizabeth, I cotton to you. We have to be careful or your family will isolate you from me. We'll have no time alone...at all." He smiled just a tad and he said, "That's probably how we'll be when our daughters are your age now."

Elizabeth watched him. "How do you know this so well?"

"I've watched how my mom and dad are." Klyn moved his hand as he continued, "My aunts and uncles, the neighbors, the strangers—everybody does it. Didn't you see your nephews watching for us?"

"Who else watches you?"

"I hate to tell you this, but *all* the Keepers are nosier than hell. It's a struggle. A young boy can't even smoke! Somebody is always watching."

Klyn sighed and mentioned, "Just because I loused up, you're ticked with me."

"Probably." Elizabeth tried to get away, then she said, "Release me."

"I would, but you'd get away. I need you with me." He smiled a tad and licked his lips as he watched her withdrawal.

Elizabeth said, "It's too soon. This isn't real. We should forget it."

"Do you realize what it would be like if I serenade you under your window?" Klyn said that so earnestly. He went on, "I can't sing any good song. I sing awful songs that cowboys sing to horses and cows. That's terrible. They sing through their noses."

"Men are so difficult." Elizabeth sighed.

Klyn smiled. He put a kind hand on her shoulder, but she moved her shoulder quickly, and Klyn removed his hand. He tilted his Stetson and smiled. He said, "I will see you later." And he strolled off toward his horses.

As Klyn waited for Elizabeth to come around, he continued his search for the person who shot the big, silent bullet over onto Keeper land.

He found a scouting place, across from the area where the wall of the canyon was so bare. He heard the discharges and saw the puffs of dirt as the place was shot. But the bullets were all on target. Those that didn't hit the bald face of the canyon wall didn't go far. Klyn had put up a thick wooden billboard on the land behind the bald face of the cliff.

So far, there was no serious puncture to the board. He continued to watch.

And right in front of him, Klyn saw the evidence of the big, silent bullet. He did! He hadn't heard anything, but he saw the puff. Just the puff. The bullet had struck the canyon wall but hadn't gone beyond. Where the hell had it come from?

Klyn went from house to house to house in the town. He didn't get the answers he sought, but he was invited by everybody to the dance that Saturday.

That irritated him at first, then he realized he'd be able to ask who all had done what all.

He began thanking those who'd asked, then said, "I know where it is, and I'll be there."

The inviters laughed. "We'll all look for you. We intend to convince you to live here permanently."

Klyn laughed. Elizabeth might be the first objector. He told the inviters, "I'll be there."

With that response, each local thought he was Klyn's host.

Wearing a good outfit and his Stetson, Klyn arrived at the dance on Saturday. Almost everybody knew who he was, and they insisted on introducing him to those he hadn't met yet. But he ended up meeting some of the same people several times. And one of them was the young woman whose name was...Elizabeth Moore. Yep. There she was.

He said, "I haven't seen you for a while."

She replied easily enough. "I've been busy."

But even though she tried to appear easy, Klyn knew something was wrong still.

When people shifted and regrouped, Klyn tried to get Elizabeth alone—but it was for only a very limited time. He watched her looking away from him. He asked, "When may I call on you?"

She looked surprised. "Why do that?"

"I miss you."

"You'll recover."

"I want a formal meeting in which I'll take off my...Stetson."

She laughed despite herself.

Other men approached and asked, "What'd he say that made you laugh?"

Elizabeth replied, "He's odd."

One man gasped. "I've noticed that very thing!"

Klyn laughed. He didn't appear to mind being the culprit. The males told her impossible things about him as if he'd made every mistake in this whole land.

Her eyes danced and she licked her lips. She asked Klyn, "How did you find such... friends?"

And he replied, "Just raw luck."

They all laughed. So, of course, others came to ask, "What's so funny?"

The males already assembled replied, "Klyn's talking."

So the newcomers asked, "Okay, Klyn, what's making these guys laugh thataway?"

Klyn said seriously, "I'm trying to be serious."

That made them all laugh. Elizabeth tried to be solemn. Her eyes danced and her face flushed in humor.

Klyn watched her and he thought, My God, she is magic. How can I make her mine forever?

Ten

Elizabeth was becoming more and more convinced that it was Klyn whom she probably would love forever, but first she had something very important to tell him.

She realized he was...different. He included her in his chats with the other males. That was unusual. He was a man, but he was more conscientious of a female than just that she was...female.

She listened to the cheerful taunting of the other men, and Klyn's amused replies. He didn't mind being teased at all. He was a Keeper. And the males finally realized none of them would ever manage to get Elizabeth's attention.

She was not interested. Klyn responded wonderfully to their ribbing, and Elizabeth laughed so much that her insides ached. She glowed.

Klyn saw only Elizabeth. He had forgotten there were other people around.

She was so fragile. It was as if he needed to carry her on a silk cushion. Okay. He could do that. He smiled at her.

Why did she look so...ethereal?

He asked, "Would you like me to carry you on a silk cushion?"

At his earnest question, she laughed and put a hand to her face.

He licked his lips and smiled softly. He was caught by her.

She asked kindly, "Why do you watch me now?"

Not for the first time, Klyn thought about how this woman was his.

Then he considered. Was that what he'd thought about every woman along the way? He hadn't. *This* woman had been different.

He told Elizabeth, "Remember. I've got the first and last dance with you, and any in between that I can manage."

She grinned at him. "I remember."

So Klyn told each of the men to behave and leave Elizabeth be. Some agreed with some disgust, and one said, "I'll take my dance with her."

Klyn shook his head. "Then I'll just have to take you aside and ruin your face." He looked at the man named Theo with concern. "I'd probably hurt my fist. It would be better for us both if you just behave."

"Give me ten dollars."

Klyn took a deep breath and said with some concern, "You'll just behave." Very quietly, he added, "You hear me?"

And the man said, "Well, hell, Klyn. Let's do it my way for a change."

Klyn shook his head. "No. You'll do it for a buck, just like everybody else, or I'll change the surface of your face."

"You think you can do that?"

"Child," Klyn said with endurance, "I *know* I can. Don't try my patience. The dollar or a rearranged face. Which do you prefer?"

Theo said, "I can handle that."

"The dollar?"

Theo shook his head. "The dance."

Klyn said, "Well, I'll be darned. How come women like you?"

Theo shifted his chew over to the other side of his mouth, and a little tobacco juice leaked from the side of his mouth as he said, "I'm couth."

However, Theo finally accepted the dollar and hadn't cut in or demanded a dance with Elizabeth.

No one did.

Elizabeth said, "Nobody else has wanted to dance with me tonight. I feel abandoned."

Without looking at her, Klyn moved her around with one hand and brought her back to him with the other as he said, "I paid them to leave you be, so's I could dance with you myself."

She laughed and said, "You're kind to think of that reply."

"Honey, I never lie, nor do I pretend anything at all. I'm an honest and level man. I gave each of the guys a buck to leave you be. I had to arm wrestle several who thought you were worth more than one dollar. I did manage. I got all the dances."

She stopped. Then she tilted back her head and just laughed.

He smiled and licked his lips, but his eyes were wicked and filled with cleverness. He told her. "And I get a kiss for all this work. Any man who manages all the dances gets a kiss from the lady. That's you and you gotta kiss *me*."

"How shocking."

"You'll adjust."

She put back her head to laugh again, but it was softly done and quite ladylike.

He told her, "You're just lucky I talked Theo into taking the dollar and not the ten he requested. He doesn't bathe and he chews tobacco!"

"No!"

"Yep. You need some man to protect you, and you're lucky you've got me." He looked sly. He told her, "You're a trial to a man."

Elizabeth stopped dancing and was very serious. "Klyn, I have something very important to tell you about the silent bullets you're investigating."

Klyn looked at Elizabeth seriously. He asked, "Are *you* shooting over the canyon?"

"No—" She moved her hands helplessly. "But nothing happens around here. People get bored. Many fire bullets into the side of the canyon. My…grandfather fires bullets into the canyon. And I recently learned they are silent.''

Klyn was shocked and just looked at her as they stood in the middle of the dance floor, facing each other, excessively serious. ''Your grandfather fires off silent bullets across the canyon?'' Klyn couldn't believe it.

Very seriously, Elizabeth nodded.

He said, ''And some don't hit the wall of the canyon? Do you know how far they go?''

''Off into the woods,'' she said.

''How far?'' Klyn was very serious and appalled.

Elizabeth considered. ''I'm not sure. A hundred feet?''

''No, they go about two miles. I'll take you across the canyon and let you see for yourself.''

Elizabeth asked, ''Is this a lure to get me into the boondocks?''

Klyn shook his head as his eyes stayed on her. He said, ''It will be interesting for you. If you'd like to take along some other women, or who all, it would be okay.''

Elizabeth said seriously, ''Whoever you'd like along will be fine with me.''

Klyn chose an interesting set of observers to go along. He chose people who were known as

being honest. He had chosen from all those men
and women he'd become acquainted with. And
they were interested and serious. They mentioned that they loved Elizabeth Moore, and
Klyn had better be sure what he was doing.

He replied each time, "We'll see."

But he was very grim. He was a little sick.
He felt odd.

One of the women told him, "Even if she or
her family *did* do something like that, it
wouldn't have been deliberately."

Klyn glanced at the woman stoically, and he
said nothing. He was still in shock. It couldn't
be Elizabeth or her family. It couldn't be.

The journey took a while as the group went
down into the canyon and found a place to cross
the river. As they went up the other side of the
canyon, they walked their horses along the lip
of the bullet-blanketed portion of the cliff's fa-
cade.

How strange it was for the Pleasant natives to
be on land they'd fired on. They looked back on
their town from an angle they'd not seen. They
found places they knew and, of course, they

found their own homes. They exclaimed over what all they could see.

Klyn had no out. The people were there, on horses, and they had been asked to see this situation. And it was a hell of one! Even worse was the fact that they were becoming more and more interested in the views and delighted at being where they were.

Klyn had thought they'd stay serious and observing.

Naw.

They began with "Oh!" and then they looked and pointed and shared.

Klyn considered that when they finally found all the dried, white bones of the killed animals, the mood would change.

Then he looked at Elizabeth. And he was dismayed he'd done such a thing as to drag her out on a horse into an area where other people would see what all her people had done to the Keepers.

He was appalled they would see it all.

He became silent, drew back and let them all go ahead of him.

They moved their horses onto Keeper land as they looked at the thick wooden stopper, which Klyn had erected behind the top of the cliff in the trees. There was one great bullet embedded in the wood.

Pointing at the bullet, Elizabeth gasped, "That's my granddaddy's bullet! I'm glad you got it stopped so soon. It could have gone into the trees and scared the birds."

In Klyn's mind he wondered who ever thought of the bullets hitting…birds?

Klyn took them farther along the way, and they saw the bones of the killed animals. They asked, "What happened to those creatures?"

Klyn said, "Look closer. They were shot."

And, sure enough, it was true.

The group exclaimed, but as they rode along and saw more bones—with bullets—they became quiet. They looked and frowned.

Elizabeth got off her horse and looked at the bullets. She turned her concerned face up to Klyn and said, "These are our bullets." She stood up and looked around in silence. She said, "Did the animals walk back here to die?"

Klyn told her, "They died here."

"The bullets came this far?"

And Klyn told her, "Farther."

Silently, they rode their horses along the trail of the bullets. At one point, Klyn told her, "That is where our 'guest' clipped the fence and came inside Keeper territory. His horse was killed by one of your bullets.''

Elizabeth looked at Klyn seriously and said nothing.

They rode farther into Keeper land. Klyn pointed out the place where Tom's horse had been startled by the sound of the big bullet...and left Tom with a broken leg and arm.

Everyone was silent. They looked and frowned. They all knew the bullets had come from Elizabeth's granddaddy's gun.

Elizabeth turned back and counted the skeletons. She wrote down how many it was. It was a lot. She looked at the bones. She told Klyn, ''My family needs to reimburse you all for the cattle that were killed. We beg your pardon.''

He watched her as she went ahead, returning to the canyon.

One man from the group went up and rode alongside her. He was an older man and he didn't say anything to her, he was just there. One of the women rode up on the other side of Elizabeth.

Pretty soon, Klyn was left behind, trailing and alone. Everyone else was up around the silent

Elizabeth, and nobody said anything to anyone else.

It was extraordinarily pensive.

Probably the most anguished was Klyn. He should have done things some other way. He'd goofed. He loved this woman. But he figured his chances with her were now zero. He went into a blue funk.

When they got to town, the people angled off with a touch to Elizabeth's shoulder, but no words.

By the time they got to the Moores' place, only Klyn was following her. Elizabeth got off his horse and said, "I appreciate the use of your horse, and I'm very sorry to have harmed and killed the Keeper creatures. I'll see your uncle and tell him so. Goodbye."

She turned away.

Klyn said, "Wait!" He wasn't entirely sure what he wanted to say, if anything. He couldn't let her leave him when she was this upset. He said, "You had to know."

"Yeah," she agreed.

"What if Tom had been killed?"

Tears filled her eyes and she ignored them. She said, "Yes."

Klyn told her, "I didn't mean to embarrass you. It was something you didn't even know was happening."

She looked down at her fingers. "I know, but that doesn't change what's happened."

Klyn told her, "I love you, Elizabeth."

She nodded but did not reply or look at him.

He said, "We had to find out who was killing my uncle's animals…and his son was harmed."

She buried her face in her hands and just bawled.

In a flash, Klyn was off his horse to hold her against him. "I should have just taken you over there so that you could understand."

Her words wobbly, she told him, "The others need to know." She looked up with such despair. "I had no idea Grandpa's silent bullets shot so far."

"Did he shoot it?"

"All of us did."

"Didn't you have any idea at all how far the bullets went?"

And she exclaimed, "We couldn't see where the bullets went!"

"Somebody in my family has been over here how many times, trying to find out who was responsible."

"We never met them. I'll go see them."

And Klyn said, "I'll go with you."

Turning away, she said, "You need not be involved. I'll tell them what happened all along." Then she looked at him with her tear-filled eyes.

He was devastated.

She asked, "Who should I see first?"

He watched her. He told her, "They'll forgive you right away."

"They'll be furious!"

He moved restlessly. "They've been irritated all along. They'll be relieved it's over." Then he said, "Elizabeth—" But he didn't know how to go on.

She turned and looked at him. She said, "I understand." Then she walked away in such degradation that he was truly wobbled.

Everybody in town was wobbled! Who could be shocked or angry at Elizabeth? They gathered around her and were with her relentlessly.

Her grandfather was shocked the bullets were fatal to animals. Her family became hostile to the Keepers. Elizabeth told the family to quit and think straight.

How could the town be angry with Klyn?

He'd been trying to solve the case of the dead animals.

Everybody was on her family's side! But they did understand that the Keepers were concerned for their stock...and that one of their own had almost been killed. That had wobbled everybody.

So Klyn went onto Elizabeth's front porch and just sat.

She came out and said a bit wobbly, "You ought to go on home and rest."

He looked up at her and said, "I can't. I've got to be here with you."

She took a careful breath and said, "I'm not good company."

He said, "I'm going with you to the Keepers."

"No. I can go by myself."

"I'm going with you."

She was patient. "I believe I'd rather go alone."

Yet again he said, "I'm going with you."

She said, "No."

He said, "Yes."

Elizabeth gave up and went into the house. She didn't invite him inside. Klyn took out his cellular phone and called his uncle John. They exchanged greetings. Then Klyn sat back and looked out over the fields to the canyon and told his uncle the whole damned mess.

Just about all Uncle John Keeper said was "Oh." He said a whole *lot* of "Oh's." Then he told Klyn, "Come over with her and—"

Klyn interrupted, "She wants this meet with you to be alone."

There was a pause, then his uncle sighed and said, "I'll put a couple of clean handkerchiefs in my pockets."

"I'll be around."

John Keeper said, "I thought you said she'd be here by herself."

"I'll be there."

John laughed softly. "I wish my brother would have let me have you right away."

"You have enough kids."

John said to Klyn, "You know we won't harm her or scold her."

"That's the only reason I'm letting her come over."

John laughed. "That's a good Keeper."

So two days later, Mrs. Keeper, Senior, held Elizabeth in her arms and hugged her nicely. She said, "What a delight to meet you!"

Elizabeth said immediately, "I'm sorry about the animals."

"My dear, you have no idea how many times I've wanted to assassinate those nasty creatures—and some of the humans."

"But you didn't!"

"I just haven't had the time!"

Elizabeth smiled at Mrs. Keeper's attempt at humor.

John Keeper was cordial and expressed no grief in losing all those animals through the years.

Elizabeth explained exactly what had happened. She was so upset. She wanted to pay for the replacement of the animals killed.

John looked at his wife and bit back a smile. He told Elizabeth, "You have to know we have vultures? They're hungry and they were delighted to get the carrion."

The Keepers soothed the anxious Elizabeth. They declined taking any money from her. They told her their son Tom was fine and that the flocks of the various animals were about out of hand. They lied wonderfully.

Klyn had to wait until they were married to make love with his beautiful Elizabeth again.

She stayed with his uncle and aunt, and it was they who arranged the wedding.

They did contact Elizabeth's family, but it was interesting how well Mrs. Keeper, Senior, arranged things her way.

All the Keepers and Moores showed up for the wedding. It was a madhouse of talk and laughter...and forgiveness.

Later that night when the honeymooners were in bed, sated and happy, Klyn said, "I've got you now, you know. Once I was afraid this might not happen."

Elizabeth smiled really smug. "You cotton to me. So you think you'll keep me?"

"Ahhhhhh, yes, Mrs. Keeper. I'll love you and keep you forever."

* * * * *

THANK YOU FOR SHOPPING AT THE
BOOK RACK. PLEASE COME AGAIN.

Silhouette® Desire.

is proud to present a brand-new miniseries by bestselling author

LEANNE BANKS

Meet the Logans— each a sexy blend of power, brains and strength. But what each Logan seeks most is that one great love that lasts a lifetime....

On sale January 2000—**HER FOREVER MAN**
On sale March 2000—**THE DOCTOR WORE SPURS**
On sale May 2000—**EXPECTING HIS CHILD**

Look for all three of these irresistible stories of love, heading your way in 2000—only from

Where love comes alive™

Available at your favorite retail outlet.

Visit us at www.romance.net   SDLL

Looking For More Romance?

Visit Romance.net

Look us up on-line at: http://www.romance.net

Check in daily for these and other exciting features:

Hot off the press

View all current titles, and purchase them on-line.

What do the stars have in store for you?

Horoscope

Hot deals

Exclusive offers available only at Romance.net

Plus, don't miss our interactive quizzes, contests and bonus gifts.

PWEB

Don't miss Silhouette's newest cross-line promotion,

Four royal sisters find their own Prince Charmings as they embark on separate journeys to find their missing brother, the Crown Prince!

The search begins
in October 1999 and
continues through February 2000:

On sale October 1999: **A ROYAL BABY ON THE WAY**
by award-winning author **Susan Mallery** (Special Edition)

On sale November 1999: **UNDERCOVER PRINCESS**
by bestselling author **Suzanne Brockmann** (Intimate Moments)

On sale December 1999: **THE PRINCESS'S WHITE KNIGHT**
by popular author **Carla Cassidy** (Romance)

On sale January 2000: **THE PREGNANT PRINCESS**
by rising star **Anne Marie Winston** (Desire)

On sale February 2000: **MAN...MERCENARY...MONARCH**
by top-notch talent **Joan Elliott Pickart** (Special Edition)

ROYALLY WED
Only in—
SILHOUETTE BOOKS

Available at your favorite retail outlet.

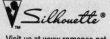

Visit us at www.romance.net

SSERW

Desire

These women are about to find out what happens
when they are forced to wed the men of their dreams
in **Silhouette Desire's** new series promotion:

The Bridal Bid

Look for
the bidding to begin
in **December 1999** with:

GOING…GOING…WED! (SD #1265)
by **Amy J. Fetzer**

And look for
THE COWBOY TAKES A BRIDE (SD#1271)
by **Cathleen Galitz** in **January 2000:**

Don't miss the next book in this series,
MARRIAGE FOR SALE (SD #1284)
by **Carol Devine,** coming in **April 2000.**

The Bridal Bid only from **Silhouette Desire**.

Available at your favorite retail outlet.

Silhouette®
Where love comes alive™

Visit us at www.romance.net   SDTBB2

The clock is ticking for three brides-to-be
in these three brand-new stories!

3, 2, 1...
Married!

In this exciting
collection of romantic tales,
three marriage-minded women set their
sights on becoming brides in time for the New Year.

How to hook a husband when time is of the essence?

Bestselling author **SHARON SALA** takes her heroine way
out west, where the men are plentiful...and more than
willing to make some lucky lady a "Miracle Bride."

Award-winning author **MARIE FERRARELLA** tells the
story of a single woman searching for any excuse to
visit the playground and catch sight of a member of
"The Single Daddy Club."

Beloved author **BEVERLY BARTON** creates a heroine
who discovers that personal ads are a bit like opening
Door Number 3—the prize for "Getting Personal" may
just be more than worth the risk!

On sale December 1999, at your favorite retail outlet.
Only from Silhouette Books!

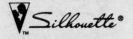
Silhouette ®

Visit us at www.romance.net   PS321

MONTANA MAVERICKS

Big Sky Brides

Legendary love comes to Whitehorn, Montana,
once more as beloved authors

Christine Rimmer, Jennifer Greene and Cheryl St.John

present three brand-new stories in this exciting anthology!

Meet the Brennan women:

SUZANNA, DIANA and ISABELLE

Strong-willed beauties who find unexpected
love in these irresistible marriage of
covnenience stories.

Don't miss
MONTANA MAVERICKS: BIG SKY BRIDES
On sale in February 2000,
only from Silhouette Books!

Available at your favorite retail outlet.

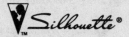

Visit us at www.romance.net   PSMMBSB

**Start celebrating Silhouette's 20th anniversary
with these 4 special titles by
New York Times bestselling authors**

Fire and Rain*
by Elizabeth Lowell

King of the Castle
by Heather Graham Pozzessere

State Secrets*
by Linda Lael Miller

Paint Me Rainbows*
by Fern Michaels

On sale in December 1999

Plus, a special free book offer inside each title!

Available at your favorite retail outlet
*Also available on audio from Brilliance.

Silhouette®
Where love comes alive™

Visit us at www.romance.net   PSNYT_R

**Special Edition is celebrating
Silhouette's 20th anniversary!**

Special Edition brings you:

• brand-new LONG, TALL TEXANS
Matt Caldwell: Texas Tycoon by **Diana Palmer**
(January 2000)

• a bestselling miniseries
PRESCRIPTION: MARRIAGE
(December 1999-February 2000)
Marriage may be just what the doctor ordered!

• a brand-new miniseries SO MANY BABIES
(January-April 2000)
At the Buttonwood Baby Clinic,
lots of babies—and love—abound

• the exciting conclusion of ROYALLY WED!
(February 2000)

• the new AND BABY MAKES THREE:
THE DELACOURTS OF TEXAS
by **Sherryl Woods**
(December 1999, March & July 2000)

And on sale in June 2000, don't miss
Nora Roberts' brand-new story
Irish Rebel
in **Special Edition.**

Available at your favorite retail outlet.

Silhouette®
Where love comes alive™

Visit us at www.romance.net   PS20SSE_R